AFTER *the* GOLD RUSH

AFTER the GOLD RUSH

To Wendy
Wm. Stanley

WILLIAM STANLEY

Copyright © 2024 William Stanley.

All rights reserved. No part of this book may be used or reproduced by any means, graphic, electronic, or mechanical, including photocopying, recording, taping or by any information storage retrieval system without the written permission of the author except in the case of brief quotations embodied in critical articles and reviews.

This is a work of fiction. All of the characters, names, incidents, organizations, and dialogue in this novel are either the products of the author's imagination or are used fictitiously.

Archway Publishing books may be ordered through booksellers or by contacting:

Archway Publishing
1663 Liberty Drive
Bloomington, IN 47403
www.archwaypublishing.com
844-669-3957

Because of the dynamic nature of the Internet, any web addresses or links contained in this book may have changed since publication and may no longer be valid. The views expressed in this work are solely those of the author and do not necessarily reflect the views of the publisher, and the publisher hereby disclaims any responsibility for them.

Any people depicted in stock imagery provided by Getty Images are models, and such images are being used for illustrative purposes only. Certain stock imagery © Getty Images.

Interior Image Credit: Astrid Ackerman

ISBN: 978-1-6657-5657-0 (sc)
ISBN: 978-1-6657-5658-7 (e)

Library of Congress Control Number: 2024902810

Print information available on the last page.

Archway Publishing rev. date: 02/19/2024

DEDICATION

In memory of my loving sister, Hilda, who was always there when I needed her.

DAWSON

BEV'S FUNERAL

Beverly was an Indigenous woman who lived her entire life in the Dawson area. A respected elder in her tribe, she had a home situated on fifty acres of forested land. In her younger years, she had served as a midwife for her tribe, assisting in the birth of many children. Bev, as she was known, had been a widow for many years, with no children of her own. Perhaps this is why she doted on her extended family, treating all of them as if she had birthed them. In addition to caring deeply for her own, she also spent many years assisting tribe members who fell on hard times. Her generosity was legendary, as were her skills in the kitchen.

In her later years, Bev reminded everyone she met of a sweet grandmother, always welcoming them into her home and willing to offer sage advice. Her spirit shone like a beacon of light to the weary and downtrodden she encountered. She fed and nourished the spirits of the hungry in her tribe and hosted large gatherings at Christmas. Bev seemed to have boundless energy, but unbeknown to her family and friends, she had been fighting an illness she did not understand.

One night in the spring, Bev passed peacefully in her

sleep, joining her husband who had been waiting patiently for her in the afterlife. Living in the forest as fur trappers, existed a community of young couples who were all related to Bev. She treated these young adults like her children, helping them out financially if needed and hosting family events, such as weddings and parties at Christmas. Losing Bev was like losing their own mother, an event the fur trappers and their children would never get over.

Bev was buried on her property, in the same small cemetery where her husband was interred. A crowd of two hundred mourners attended her service, watching as her body was lowered into the cold ground. Bev is now but a thought of days past, a woman never forgotten and sorely missed in this land of sad memories.

CHAPTER ONE

The winds of change were sweeping over Dawson. Many wives and children in the lower forty-eight waited for their men to come back from the goldfields, however not all these hapless prospectors ever returned to their families. Unprepared, some men died at the hands of nature or their fellow man, their bodies left in the forests of the Yukon to be eaten by the predators and scavengers which called this land home. Some men, hearing of a new strike in Alaska, packed up their gear and headed to try their luck in a new area. And some, tired of chasing gold, decided it was time to go home, their dreams crushed by the relentless hardships they faced daily to quench their thirst of yellow fever. The population of Dawson began to dwindle as these gold hunters moved on.

Wendy, Jason, and their son, Kuzih, had moved from their cabin in the wilderness to Bev's house in Dawson. A prior verbal agreement between Wendy and her Aunt Bev had been further cemented as fact in Bev's will, which stated Jason and Wendy would inherit the house upon her passing. The stipulations of this agreement included their responsibility to care for the donkeys in the barn and allow family members living in the forest to freely use the pack animals as needed. Bev also stated it was very important for Wendy and Jason to continue hosting Christmas celebrations, inviting their fellow trappers in the bush to their new home each year. These terms would be honoured by Wendy and Jason, who had taken up residence in the house.

In addition to taking over Bev's home, a sizable amount of money had been left to Jason and Wendy to keep the old estate running, ensuring the structures did not get dilapidated and left to lay in ruins. When Wendy and Jason moved into the house, they assumed Bev's duties feeding the poor with donated meat kept in the large outdoor freezers on her property. Tribe members continued to drop off game when it was available, to ensure no member of their tribe went hungry.

Because of the upheaval Bev's death brought to Jason and Wendy's lives, they desperately needed a break. This coming summer, the couple hoped to take a one-week canoe trip, without their son, down a tributary of the Yukon River. Final decisions would be made later regarding this trip; for now, it was something they both looked forward to.

Wendy walked to the barn to feed Omar, Honey, and Baby Jack. She loved feeding the donkeys, which belonged to various relatives and were boarded at Bev's barn. When alone with these animals, memories of Bev flooded Wendy's consciousness, pleasant thoughts about her favorite aunt, never to be forgotten.

CHAPTER TWO

After moving to Dawson, Wendy and Jason gave their larger cabin in the bush to Johnathan and Shining Star, Wendy's cousin, and her husband. The couple appreciated having more living space for their child, Grey Eagle. The mattresses in their new cabin were made from goose down, a far cry and more comfortable to sleep on than the ones filled with straw at their previous cabin. This left Jonathan and Shining Star's cabin empty. Those buildings needed to be maintained or they would be taken over by nature in a very short time.

It was agreed that Wendy and Jason would find an appropriate couple to move into the vacant home, something Bev would have wanted them to do. She had prided herself on providing a helpful start for newcomers in the bush, although nothing quite as grand as gifting someone an entire homestead. Ownership of a habitable cabin would be a gift never expected by the receiver and one that would give a pair of new arrivals a head start. Wendy would wait for the perfect candidates to come along, before offering the cabin as a gift to start their married life. This was a prerequisite for receiving the cabin, that it be a wedding gift to a young couple, an act of kindness to assure they got off to a successful start living together, where they longed to be.

The bright but distant sunshine slowly melted the snow. Another winter would soon be over, and life would return to the Yukon. The ice on lakes in the area would soon thaw, allowing the migratory waterfowl to return, where they would breed and carry on their lifeline. These events allowed trappers, who inhabited cabins on the lakes, to harvest numerous waterfowl for food over the summer months.

The snow was slowly melting from around Wendy and Jason's house and barn. The first shoots of green appeared from the ground hugging the buildings, proving the sun's ability to bring life back from death. Jason was expecting Joe and Mary, friends who were considered family, to visit Dawson soon, as they would be coming to pick up Honey. In the early spring, before the ground became muddy, the couple used Honey, one of the family's pack animals, for completing chores around their cabin. While staying with Joe and Mary, Honey would be kept in their sturdy fur shed, before being returned to Dawson, where she was housed in a locked barn.

These were not the same privileges Honey's mate, Omar, enjoyed when he was taken out in the bush. This donkey felt he was given no security in regard for his life, always fearful that someday he would end up as dinner. He envisioned being dragged off into the bush to be eaten, never to see his wife and child in Dawson again. Omar would rather retire his position and spend the rest of his life in the safety of the barn, a dream which had little chance of becoming reality.

CHAPTER THREE

Wendy and Jason had moved to Dawson last summer, taking possession of Bev's house at the beginning of June, after her estate was settled. They carried their personal belongings with them from their cabin, leaving the rest of their belongings behind. The couple moved the items they wanted to keep to Dawson this past winter, when they could use their dog team for transportation. Jonathan and Shining Star had moved into Wendy and Jason's cabin shortly after they moved to Dawson. Their old cabin lay empty for now, but the couple hoped someone would take possession of the building soon.

The day in Dawson was sunny and warm. The early April sun was melting the snow which covered the ground. A constant dripping from the roofs of the homes in Dawson could be heard when walking down the muddy streets. The crowds were mostly gone, as the lure of finding gold in the Klondike had diminished. The fervid gold seekers had lost interest in the area, heading to a new discovery of this precious metal in Alaska, starting a new gold rush on American soil. Others had given up completely and returned home.

With little fanfare, Joe and Mary arrived at Wendy and Jason's property. They checked on Honey before heading to the house and being graciously welcomed by Wendy and Jason. They invited the couple inside, and while sitting at the table drinking coffee, talked about Jason and Wendy's past and how their lives had changed since moving into town. The number of permanent residents in Dawson was growing. During the heyday of the gold rush, investment had poured into Canada's most northern city. People who were successful finding gold took a liking to the lifestyle, deciding to stay in the north to live. Some built homes and business expanded, allowing Dawson to grow into a larger and more enduring place.

After an influx of rowdy men flooded into Dawson, a new law enforcement agency was sent to maintain order. A permanent outpost was built and the North West Mounted Police became a presence in the area. Using Dawson as their permanent location, they built small wooden shelters throughout the bush for overnight stays. Equipped with a woodstove and beds to sleep on, these buildings provided shelter when policing the cabins built in the forest. One of the Mounties' priorities was the safety of the fur trappers living outside of town. Too many men were dying alone in the bush, unaware of the dangers of cabin fever, failing to get out before insanity took over their minds.

The Mounties had made a big difference in law and order in Dawson, preventing many serious crimes from taking place. The citizens were glad to have law enforcement on their side and hoped for a peaceful existence going forward, unlike their chaotic past at the height of the gold rush.

CHAPTER FOUR

Joe and Mary were invited to spend the night, and being in no hurry to go back to their cabin, they accepted Jason and Wendy's offer of dinner, followed by a friendly card game. Outside the cabin it was raining. The storm had started a short time ago and had not stopped, turning the snow into slush on the trails. Joe felt he had missed the opportunity to use Honey for help around his cabin. The weather in the Yukon had warmed earlier than expected, turning the landscape into a mucky mess. This made travel difficult, especially with a donkey. Joe would leave Honey in Dawson until the trails dried up, which would make the ground easier for the pack animal to walk on. Traversing through too much mud would tire the animal to the point of exhaustion, making her refuse to move further. Being left with a stubborn donkey who won't move, even under threat, is not a place Joe wanted to be.

Wendy and Mary prepared dinner, while the men took Jason's son, Kuzih, into the living room to play with the family pets, King and Rusty. Kuzih laughed when the dogs rolled over, wanting their bellies rubbed. Jason put Kuzih on King's back, making the child laugh hysterically as Joe led King around the living room, with him holding on tight.

The women called their husbands for dinner, with the dogs being the first ones at the table. With easier access to commodities, such as flour, Wendy could now prepare meals with baked bread and other goodies fresh from her hot oven. Shortages of goods in Dawson were less acute, with not as many people competing for the limited number of supplies available at that time. Jason had shot some grouse the day before Joe and Mary arrived, which was what was being served for dinner. He took the dogs outside and fed them some whitefish he had caught through the still thick ice on the lake. He left the animals outdoors, while the couples ate dinner.

Pleasant conversations between the diners took place for the next hour. Jason and Wendy told Joe and Mary of their desire to take a one-week canoe trip this summer. Mary offered to come to town and watch Kuzih and their dogs while they were away. With their son being older, Wendy and Jason would not worry about turning this responsibility over to their trusted friends.

After dinner, the couples retired to the living room for coffee and hot bread covered in butter, cinnamon, and sugar. At times, it was possible to find odd items on the shelves of the general store. Such was the case when Wendy found cinnamon, with no explanation as to how it found its way to Dawson.

The sky had cleared, revealing moonlight shining through the windows of the house. The couples looked outside, watching their dogs frolicking in the front yard, as a million shining stars twinkled in the night sky. The couples sat around the table, teaching each other new card games and enjoying the warm friendship they shared together. The group played cards until sleepiness overtook them. Unable to fight it off, they all turned in for the night, where a quiet night's sleep would be offset by a chaotic day tomorrow.

CHAPTER FIVE

Joe and Mary were awakened in the middle of the night by distant barking from dogs in Dawson. A short time later, Mary urged Joe to pull himself out of bed to investigate this unusual activity. Joe walked to the window and looked out in the direction of Dawson, where flames and smoke were clearly visible in the night sky. Wendy and Jason entered the room, joining Joe at the window. They watched for a few seconds, at what appeared to be a house burning down. Joe and Jason dressed quickly and walked twenty minutes into Dawson to see what was burning and if they could be of help.

Upon arrival, the men noticed a crowd gathered around what was now a pile of smoldering ruins. The captain of the Dawson fire battalion told Jason a charred body had been removed from the ruins of the wooden building. Many of the house fires at the time were caused by unsafe stove pipes or accidents with burning lamps, usually resulting in the building burning to the ground. At times, the dwellings' owners lost their lives before being able to escape.

The fire battalion chief told Joe and Jason they were lucky this fire had not spread to any of the nearby structures.

After the fire of 1899, which destroyed over 110 buildings in town, any building fire in town was considered dangerous. Many residents still clung to the habit of soaking blankets in water and hanging them from their exterior walls to encase their homes in ice, hoping to prevent fire from spreading to them.

The men returned to the house and told their wives what happened in town. The couples decided to go back to bed for two more hours of sleep. Joe and Mary left for home with Rusty early in the morning, even though the conditions for the walk home were unfavorable. The terrain was wet and muddy, as the melting snow turned to liquid daily. The warm spring sunshine thawing the frozen ground was making conditions for walking difficult, but not impossible. The usual three hour walk home from Dawson took over four hours, travelling along the same route.

Upon returning home, Joe and Mary immediately noticed the lake. The ice was breaking up along the shoreline, leaving large areas of open water. Joe and Mary looked skyward, responding to the sound of honking geese. The geese were returning from their migration south, with some staying for the summer to breed and raise their young here. Many young geese were lost to predators, such as raptors, fish, and even raccoons, who ate the goslings as a healthy snack.

Reaching the cabin, Mary pointed out a mother fox and her two young, lying under a large evergreen tree in their front yard. Startled by Rusty, the small canines bolted into the protection of the forest. Joe restrained Rusty, so he would not run down the younger foxes and hurt them. Mary also noticed tiny wildflowers blooming in the sunshine, along the outer wall of their cabin, happy to see a sure sign of spring.

The couple entered the cabin and started a fire to warm the inside of the dank and cold structure. After the long and difficult walk from Dawson, Joe and Mary were looking forward to sitting and drinking hot coffee. The quiet forest and the remaining snow spread across the land would soon be gone, replaced by a greener environment, signalling the rebirth of life in the Yukon.

CHAPTER SIX

A few days later, Jason was up early. He had answered a knock at his front door to find a man who had stopped by looking for his lost dog. Jason liked the man and invited him inside, introducing him to Wendy. The trio sat down in the kitchen, having coffee together. The man said his name was Samuel, but people called him Sam. He told the couple he lived in Dawson and his husky had disappeared two days ago. Sam told Jason and Wendy he thought his dog had been stolen.

Stealing someone's dog was considered a serious crime in Dawson, with the perpetrator usually ending up with jail time. Sam had money, as his father had once had a large business in Portland, Oregon, designing and selling ironware household goods, such as cookware, fireplace implements, and woodstoves. Before his father died, he had sold the business. With Sam being one of only two heirs, he wound up becoming a wealthy man. He told Jason he wanted to start a similar business in Dawson, but he would not manufacture the goods, only sell the finished items. His products would be supplied by his father's old company in Portland, who would ship everything he ordered to Dawson.

He had already purchased a large lot, along with the lumber and other building materials needed to construct the new store. Sam told Jason and Wendy he expected as the number of permanent residents in Dawson grew, so would the need for the merchandise he was selling. He invited Jason to help do some carpentry work, telling him he would pay a decent salary for his labor. Jason accepted the job, telling Sam he would like to help on a part-time basis. Sam agreed, saying he had a construction crew coming from Oregon to erect the building, but an extra set of hands is always welcome on such a large project. Sam left, wishing the couple well and telling Jason he hoped to see him at the construction site. Wendy and Jason agreed Sam's new store would be a big hit among the townspeople in Dawson, being just what this growing frontier town needed.

Two days later, Jason and Wendy sighted an unkempt husky in their front yard. Thinking it could be Sam's dog, they called it by name, and it instantly ran over to the couple, tail wagging. They took the dog inside introducing him to King. After sniffing each other, King decided friendship was better than making this dog his enemy. The dog's name was Spearmint, Sam never explaining why the husky had been given that name. Spearmint was happy to be found, the odor of his owner still strong in Jason's house. Wendy fed the hungry dog, and after he finished eating, Jason returned him to his rightful owner. Sam, fearing he would never see his dog again, was elated and surprised.

CHAPTER SEVEN

Spearmint and Sam's reunion was a tearful one for Sam, as he expected his trusted companion to be gone forever. Spearmint was beside himself at the sight of his owner, smothering Sam with welcoming kisses, jumping up on him, and whining in happiness at seeing him again. Sam and Jason surmised the dog had been dognapped, taken into the bush, and held in captivity. He must have escaped his restraints, running off in the direction of home. After reaching Jason and Wendy's house, he probably detected the faint odor of his owner and decided to hang around the property for a short time. This was when Jason found him in his front yard, calling him by name to come to him. Jason told Sam he responded immediately to his name, running to him with tail wagging. Spearmint realized he had been saved, and was thankful this kind man took him home to be reunited with Sam.

Samuel offered Jason a reward for finding his lost dog, which he refused. He told Sam his reward was seeing him happily reunited with Spearmint. Jason noticed four men sawing and nailing lumber. Sam told Jason construction on his new building started yesterday and he expected to be open and well stocked with merchandise by late August. This should be a good time of the year for sales, as the people in Dawson prepared for the fall and winter seasons.

Before heading home, the two men made a plan for Jason to help with the finishing of his new building. Jason's woodworking skills were exceptional. Being gifted in this art, he would be an asset in building the cabinets and shelving Sam would need to display and store the goods he would be selling. The men shook hands goodbye, wishing each other well.

Jason left, heading home to tell his wife about returning Spearmint to Sam. He told Wendy about Sam's heartfelt gratitude for finding the only family member he had in the area. Sam had shared that while Spearmint was missing, he often thought about his late wife and was glad she didn't have to experience the loss of her companion. He had lost his wife in a canoeing accident. During a sudden and violent storm, which struck without warning, his wife was sent to a watery grave and her body was never found.

Wendy thought about this man, who had endured such a heartbreaking experience. She encouraged Jason to be Sam's friend, as he seemed to have no one close in the Dawson area. Jason thought this was a good idea, thinking the couple would invite Sam and Spearmint to their home for dinner some evening.

Jason went out to the barn to say hello to the donkeys who resided there and feed them. An excited ensemble of sound greeted Jason upon his arrival. He fed the animals some hay stored in the barn and laughed, telling the donkeys they would soon be able to graze on the new shoots of green grass which were now appearing everywhere. Only remnants of the winter's snow lay on the ground, allowing the vegetation to start growing again. This signalled a rebirth of life in this isolated place, the newly established territory with Dawson City as its capital.

CHAPTER EIGHT

After lunch, Wendy and Jason, along with their dog, King, and their son, planned on taking a walk around their property. Bev's husband had cleared a trail which wound through the fifty acres of land they were now the proud owners of. The snow was gone, with only remnants of white left deep in the forest. The trail was maintained once a year by the young men from Wendy's tribe, in appreciation for the assistance Bev, and now Wendy, gave to its members. The couple continued to allow the natives to store meat in their large outdoor freezers during the winter and use their property as a distribution point, where hungry people from the tribe could pick up food in times of need.

Jason's small family finished eating lunch and were ready for their walk. Wendy called King and they left on this beautiful northern day, following the trail into the forest. The sun was shining brightly in a cloudless sky. The large deciduous trees were still bare of leaves, but the small shrubbery growing amongst them were showing signs of new growth. Soon, a vibrant green would change the ecosystem from a land of brown to a sea of emerald. Wildflowers would bloom all summer, enveloping the forest and meadows in a soothing array of colours.

The dry leaves crackled under the feet of Wendy, Jason, and Kuzih as they continued their walk through the forest. The warm sun was drying the wet soggy landscape which had dominated the land for the previous two weeks. King bounded through the forest, chasing the occasional squirrel he came across up a tree. The chattering of discontent from these frightened animals echoed through the silent forest.

A short while later, the couple came to the lake which sat on their land. Crystal clear water, with remnants of ice still in some areas of this wilderness lake, came into view. Ducks and geese were plentiful in the lake, enjoying a good meal after returning from their long journey north. The couple were alerted by King's barking. Upon investigating, Jason came upon two piles of feathers along the shore. Obviously, a large raptor was living near the lake, eating the waterfowl when he was hungry, leaving a mound of feathers on the shoreline.

The couple walked around the lake. For part of the way, they could follow a section of trail they had cleared, which would eventually circle around and lead back to their house. The remainder of the way the couple followed a game trail, which made their walk more difficult. Their plans were to finish clearing the trail in the near future. They breathed the clean northern air, the smell of the forest overwhelming Wendy and Jason as they headed home, with King leading the way. King had adapted well living outside of town, instead of in the bush. His quality of life had improved dramatically since moving to Dawson, and he knew it was safest to stay close to home. If he did not leave the confines of Wendy and Jason's property, he was safe from most danger, a milestone any husky would dream of, but rarely attain.

CHAPTER NINE

The month of May arrived with sunshine and warm weather. Steward and Blossom, Wendy's brother and sister-in-law, were in their canoe, paddling quietly across their lake. They resided in the bush, a two day walk from Dawson, in an older fur-trapping cabin situated on a large lake. This time of the year in the Yukon, the water was full of wildlife; springtime was mating season for most mammals and birds living here. Soon, the lake will become a sanctuary for new life, with goslings and ducklings present everywhere. Fish filled the placid waters of the lake, providing food for humans and animals alike. Today, the water was calm, and the fish were plentiful.

Blossom used her skills with the net to catch as much food as the couple needed. The calm of the lake created an illusion of peace in this untamed wilderness, a land which claimed the lives of many well-meaning men and women. Steward and Blossom paddled the canoe back to their cabin, where Steward would clean the lake trout for them to eat, while saving the whitefish for his huskies.

Upon returning to their cabin, unexpected guests were waiting for them. Grey Wolf and Rose had come for a visit, canoeing across two lakes to arrive here. Rose was Wendy and Steward's cousin, who had married a fellow tribe member, Grey Wolf. They had been living in the bush for over a year, in a cabin Joe and Mary had given to them.

Rose told Blossom, since it was such a beautiful day they decided a canoe ride would make a perfect outing. Steward told Grey Wolf, he and Blossom were taking a trip to see Jason and Wendy soon. While they were gone, Tim, Steward's friend who owned the local sawmill, had agreed to care for his dogs. Steward said they were leaving in a few days and would spend one night at the lake, which was the halfway point of their journey when walking to Dawson.

Grey Wolf and Rose joined their friends inside the cabin for coffee, Grey Wolf telling Steward he was having a problem with wolves. The animals had been coming around their cabin at night, causing his sled dogs to suffer anxiety at the presence of these predators. He said he had shot and killed one wolf, but this did not deter the rest of the pack from returning the following night to continue harassing his dogs. After a lengthy visit, Grey Wolf and Rose left to return home. Steward and Blossom walked their friends to their canoe, wishing them well and a safe trip home.

Before returning to their cabin, Steward took a detour to the shed to clean the lake trout they had caught earlier. Steward and Blossom would enjoy the fish cooked over an open fire tonight for dinner. While Steward was cleaning the fish, Blossom started the fire. During the summer months, the men and women living remotely, spent most of their time outdoors, including cooking and eating around the fire. Confined to a small cabin during the winter, which becomes an almost intolerable situation, causes the residents to yearn for open spaces with only the forest and sky surrounding them. Spending as much time as possible outdoors was the preferred way to live during the warmer months.

Steward and Blossom sat around the campfire eating the succulent trout. The smoke from the burning wood drifted skyward, the smell of the fish drifting off into the forest. The couple sat around the crackling wood eating and enjoying the call of the loon. This mystical bird's call was a beautiful song, enjoyed by the couple who relished spending this peaceful time together. The couple would not be denied this moment in Canada's north, a moment they would treasure forever.

CHAPTER TEN

Tim arrived an hour after sunrise, paddling his canoe to Steward and Blossom's home. He would stay at Steward's cabin, until the couple returned from Dawson. Tim would travel home in the mornings, if he had work to do, and return for the night, staying to care for the dogs.

Steward greeted Tim at the lake, helping him pull his canoe ashore. They walked back to the cabin together, with Tim saying good morning to Blossom. He shared coffee with the couple, before leaving to go back to his sawmill. He needed to finish an order of lumber for a waiting customer, but wanted to see Steward and Blossom to ensure them he understood what his duties entailed. Steward and Blossom thanked Tim for his help, telling him they hoped they could return the favor some day.

The couple were planning to buy Tim coffee and sugar while in Dawson, as well as pay him for his work. The amount of money they paid him would depend on how long Steward and Blossom were away from home. Steward secured the cabin door and the couple left on their long walk to Dawson.

After the Gold Rush 27

The day in the Yukon was beautiful, with the sun casting its warm rays down from a clear blue sky. The trail to Dawson was clearly marked through the forest, having been trodden on many times before. The forest was displaying a mosaic of color, as life returned to this wilderness landscape. The deciduous trees were laden with heavy foliage, blocking the trail in some places. Steward and Blossom planned on walking until almost dark, stopping halfway to town, camping at a beautiful lake.

Steward shot a rabbit he spotted eating clover on the trail, the animal paying no attention to anything except the plant's tender, succulent sprouts. Steward shot the rabbit dead, and the couple would eat this food for dinner tonight, cooking it over an open fire. The day wore on, with Steward and Blossom making good time during their travels. As the late afternoon came upon them, the couple approached a shimmering body of water. They continued to the lakeshore camping site they had used during their past trips to Dawson. The spot was on a beautiful overhang, overlooking the lake.

Steward and Blossom gathered firewood for cooking and to cast light on the area where they would be staying tonight. Soon, the fire was burning, the flames shooting upward into the sky. Steward cleaned the rabbit and prepared to cook it over the campfire. It was a beautiful night for cooking and sleeping outside, under the stars.

The forest was silent, the only sounds being the crackling fire and the waves splashing against the shoreline. The sky was clear, a potpourri of stars filling the night sky, casting light on the lake and the couple's campsite. The sizzling aroma of the cooking rabbit filled the senses of the hungry couple, whose lives were like one, sitting alone together in one of nature's creations, a special place to enjoy love and peace while on Earth.

CHAPTER ELEVEN

The beautiful sun rose over the treeline which bordered the lake. The red sky, and the sun's reflection on the water, showed the true beauty of this northern wilderness Steward and Blossom lived in. The couple had specifically woken early to watch the sunrise together. They now sat holding hands, Blossom's head snuggled into Steward's shoulder. The couple watched in silence as the glowing ball of hot fire rose higher in the sky. An eagle, soaring over the lake, cried out for his mate, wanting her to join him in the search for food. The couple watched as the raptors dove from a high altitude, hitting the water and coming up with breakfast in their talons.

Steward and Blossom picked themselves up off the ground, stretching their aching bodies, sore from sleeping on the hard earth. They gathered the few belongings they carried with them and started the second half of their trip to Dawson. The couple expected to arrive at Wendy and Jason's house by mid-afternoon today.

The sun shone brightly down on the two hikers, as they walked through the meadows and forests of the Yukon. The forest was quiet, except for birdsong from their feathered friends. The birds living in the forest were looking for mates to help build their nests and make new families. Squirrels, unhappy with the couple's presence in their habitat, voiced their concerns loudly as they walked by.

When the sun was high in the sky, the couple stopped for a rest. Steward told Blossom they were three hours from their destination. After resting for a short time, the couple continued their way to Dawson, arriving without incident at Wendy and Jason's house in the afternoon. Wendy was pleasantly surprised to see her brother, Steward, and her sister-in-law, Blossom, at the door. They were always welcome faces to see, and Wendy was happy for their visit, something she and Jason always enjoyed.

The couples retreated to the living room for coffee and some fresh baked danish, smothered in Wendy's home-made raspberry jam she had preserved last summer. She had found the errant jar of jam hidden among the pickles on a shelf in the basement.

Wendy asked Blossom if she would like to help her clean out old vegetation from her flower beds and gardens, while Jason and Steward did some repair work in the barn and cleaned the donkeys' pens. When they were done, the women would join their husbands later in the barn, to visit with Omar and his family.

Steward had decided to no longer use pack animals in the bush, due to the dangers presented by the predators living there. The couple were hoping to use Jacob's services, the man in Dawson who would pick up and deliver supply orders in the bush, for a fee. This was how Steward and Blossom hoped to move the provisions they would need for the summer months from Dawson City to their cabin; dry and canned goods for themselves and their huskies were the priority. Steward planned to find Jacob tomorrow and talk to him, hoping the man was in town and not out on a job. Steward would have an answer tomorrow if these arrangements were possible.

CHAPTER TWELVE

Wendy and Blossom finished their work in the garden, then walked to the barn together to see what their husbands were doing and to visit the donkeys who lived there. Steward and Jason were finished cleaning the animals' pens and were getting ready to head back to the house when Wendy and Blossom entered. Upon hearing the women, the donkeys got excited, braying loudly. The animals always welcomed company and the handouts that came with it.

Steward and Jason proceeded to the house, while the woman visited with Omar and his happy family. Since Bev's passing, the donkeys were rarely used as pack animals, as it was difficult to protect these defenseless animals against the host of predators living in the forest. Bev's extended family had decided it was best to hire Jacob, who lived in Dawson and owned a delivery service. He had a solid reputation of being responsible and charging decent rates for transporting goods into the bush. The donkeys' owners no longer used them for moving goods, leaving the animals in Wendy and Jason's barn to enjoy a safe and peaceful life as pets.

When Wendy and Blossom finished their visit with the family of happy donkeys, the women joined their men in the house. Jason had filled the kettle with water and placed it on the cooktop of the woodstove to boil, planning to make coffee when the women returned.

The sound of the breeze rustling through the new growth covering the deciduous trees travelled through the open windows of Wendy and Jason's house. A recently built bird's nest could be seen hidden among the new leaves on a tree branch outside the kitchen window. Wendy was looking forward to watching the birds raise their family, without being seen by her feathered friends. She would enjoy viewing the progression from eggs, to chicks, to birds, ready to leave the nest, no longer dependent on their parents to keep them alive.

Wendy and Blossom began preparing a venison stew. Wendy had been given meat by a friend in Dawson, who had shot a deer and dropped some off. Jason and Steward went outside, preparing a bonfire in the firepit located outside the house. As the day was ending, the two couples ventured outside to sit around the large fire, eating the stew and freshly baked bread, right out of the oven.

The night was warm, the sky above full of stars. The flames from the fire rose high into the sky, as the hungry friends sat on large logs, around the open fire. The silhouette of the vast forest which graced the property was illuminated by the light from the stars and moon, shining down from the heavens above. The Yukon was living up to its reputation as the most peaceful place on earth to interact with nature. The companionship felt sitting around the fire would leave a memory of this visit in the minds of the couples forever.

CHAPTER THIRTEEN

The following morning dawned sunny and warm, with small cumulus clouds floating lazily through the bright blue sky. A warm breeze blowing from the south caused the leaves on the trees to shimmer in the morning sun. Steward and Blossom rose from their bed. They joined Wendy and Jason downstairs for coffee and hot rolls in the kitchen. The visiting couple were walking into Dawson this morning to find Jacob. They hoped he was home, and available to move supplies to their cabin, which was a two-day walk through the forest from Dawson.

Following Wendy's directions, Steward and Blossom were able to find Jacob's house. Two mules residing in a secure shed at the back of his property and smoke floating lazily into the sky from the chimney meant Jacob was probably home. Steward approached the man's door, knocking loudly. Jacob's dog, Bullet, was the first to respond to Steward's call, barking at full volume. Jacob shooed Bullet away from the door, opening it in response to Steward's knock. A strong odor of dog urine and feces emanated from inside Jacob's cabin; Jacob looked and smelled unbathed, like his dog, Bullet.

After the Gold Rush   35

Steward introduced himself and Blossom, telling Jacob he was Wendy's brother and she had suggested they come see him about some work they needed done. Steward told Jacob he needed a load of supplies transported by mule to his cabin, items needed to sustain him and his wife through the summer months. Jacob told Steward he was familiar with the area where his cabin was located, telling Steward what his fee would be. After agreeing to the charge, Jacob told Steward to have the items taken to Wendy and Jason's home, where he would be pick them up on a pre-arranged date and deliver them. Steward agreed to this plan, telling Jacob when he was ready to leave Dawson for home, he would get in touch to set a date for delivery. The men shook hands, agreeing to meet later.

Steward and Blossom left Jacob's house to walk back to Wendy and Jason's. Construction in Dawson was booming; new homes were being built from lumber cut by local sawmills using waterpower for energy. The mills' large saw blades cut logs into boards, which were used for building homes, outbuildings, and new businesses all over Dawson. Riverboats brought goods up the Yukon River from the lower forty-eight and the southern provinces and districts, including food during the summer months.

Steward and Blossom decided instead of returning to Wendy and Jason's home right away, the couple would instead rent a mule from the livery stable and pick up the items they needed for Jacob to deliver to their cabin. After securing the mule, the couple made their way to the new general store, which was built last year. Seeing it well-stocked with usable goods, the couple bought most of the merchandise they needed there. The remainder of the supplies were picked up at the mercantile store. All these goods were then taken to Wendy and Jason's and stored there. Jacob would pick them up and deliver them in the bush when the two men agreed on a date.

After finishing their use for the mule, Blossom and Steward returned the animal to the stable. On their way back to Wendy and Jason's, they stopped by Jacob's and set a date for delivery. The couple finally made it back to Wendy's just in time for dinner, happy to be done for the day, but hungry and tired in spirit.

CHAPTER FOURTEEN

Steward and Blossom woke to the sound of thunder; an intense storm was passing over Dawson. Flashes of lightning lit up the dawn, with thunder, sounding like a drum roll, reverberating across the early morning sky. A relentless downpour of rain hit the roof of the house, keeping everyone awake who were trying to sleep. The storm soon passed, leaving the forest quiet again.

Steward and Blossom decided to get out of bed. The couple went downstairs and added wood to the dying embers in the wood stove. Blossom placed a kettle of water on the cooktop to make coffee. Wendy and Jason, also awakened by the storm, came downstairs and joined Steward and Blossom in the kitchen. The bright sun was rising, spreading its warm glow across this special land.

Today, Steward and Blossom were leaving on their long trek back to their cabin. After enjoying coffee with their hosts and gathering up their belongings, the couple said goodbye and left for home. Jason had planned to help his new friend, Samuel, by doing some carpentry work at the new store he was building in Dawson. Jason kissed his wife goodbye and started walking toward town, leaving the house shortly after Steward and Blossom. He planned to meet Samuel at the work site, and spend all day building shelving for the inside of Sam's new ironware store.

Smoke rose from the numerous chimneys in town, as a cold front had passed through the area during the night. Jason reached the build site, finding the work crew already on the job. Upon seeing Jason, Samuel walked over to greet him. He discussed how the construction project was going with Jason, saying how pleased he was with the men he had hired. The foundation and exterior walls of the building were completed, and construction of the roof was set to begin.

Samuel explained to Jason what he needed him to do. Jason started working, cutting lumber to the proper sizes for the shelving needed to display Sam's merchandise inside the store. Jason's day passed quickly, as he enjoyed the comradeship with the other men he was working with. While living in isolation in a lonely cabin deep in the forest, working as a fur trapper, he had missed the company of other people. Jason was glad that hard existence was now behind him. Living in Dawson made for an easier and safer life, than trying to survive in the wilds of the Yukon.

Jason finished his workday, happy with his accomplishments, with Sam asking him to return and work another day. Samuel also mentioned to Jason he would like to stop by the house to talk with him and Wendy about a lucrative proposition he had for them. The men agreed to meet tomorrow after dinner, with Jason curious as to what Sam had in mind.

CHAPTER FIFTEEN

The winds of change were sweeping over Dawson; a building boom was going on in this isolated frontier town. New homes and businesses were being built to accommodate the growing population arriving daily. Some men who participated in the Klondike gold rush, had fallen in love with the Yukon. The lure of solitude and tranquility drew them back to Dawson, where it all began; only the hardiest of men and women would stay. For some, the far north would become their permanent home.

The following evening, Wendy answered a knock at her front door. It was Samuel, the man who was building the new ironware store. He had told Jason the day before he had something to discuss with him and his wife. Wendy invited Sam inside, where they joined Jason in the living room. Wendy made coffee, wondering what this visit was about.

After serving the coffee, along with some freshly baked cookies, Wendy seated herself beside Jason on the couch. Sam told Wendy and Jason he was looking for someone he could trust to travel to Skagway to oversee the transfer of the merchandise he had purchased to stock his new store in Dawson. Sam wanted his order checked against the manifest, before the goods left the port in Alaska. He also wanted his goods accompanied by the couple from Skagway back to Dawson, to ensure nothing was lost or stolen along the way.

Sam left Wendy and Jason's home with no definite answer from the couple as to whether they would take this job or not. Jason told Sam they would think about it and give him their answer by week's end. Samuel left the house, saying goodbye and telling the couple he was looking forward to hearing from them. Wendy and Jason both wanted to think about what Sam had asked and would discuss this potential adventure later. In the meantime, the couple laughed at their dog, King, sleeping by the fireplace, his snoring filling the living room with sound.

The rest of the evening passed by peacefully, luring the tired couple to bed early. Tomorrow would bring change into Wendy and Jason's lives, as a new tenant would be found for Johnathan and Shining Star's vacant cabin. Another young Indigenous couple wanted to try their hand living independently from the tribe and met the strict conditions Wendy had placed on receiving ownership of this wilderness home. The recently married couple had heard about the dwelling from a tribal elder and were travelling to Dawson to talk to Wendy about the well-kept cabin in the bush. During the past year it had been sitting vacant, with regular maintenance done by Johnathan to keep it habitable.

The following day around lunch time, the couple arrived from their village located in the bush. They introduced themselves to Wendy and Jason as White Dove and Black Hawk. White Dove told Wendy they were not related by blood, but they were all one people. Wendy and Jason liked the sincerity of the young couple and felt they were the right fit for Johnathan and Shining Star's old cabin. White Dove and Black Hawk wept with joy when Wendy told them the cabin was theirs. The young couple would return to their camp, collect their personal belongings and their dog, and return to Dawson in a week. Jason would then take them to their new home, where they would begin a new life together, as one.

CHAPTER SIXTEEN

Wendy and Jason sat in their living room discussing Samuel's proposal about travelling to Skagway for him. The couple decided on taking the job, but before committing themselves, they needed to find someone to stay at their house. Jason's dogs and the animals living in the barn needed to be taken care of. Joe and Mary had offered to watch Kuzih, their son, when they had previously mentioned taking a canoe trip this summer. Wendy and Jason thought the couple would be happy staying at their home in Dawson. Without any animals to care for at their own home, Mary and Joe would be able to stay in town for an extended period. With these thoughts in mind, the couple retired to bed.

The evening was warm, so Jason opened the windows of their bedroom. The gentle breeze rustled the leaves in the treetops surrounding their home. The mournful call of the loon from the lake located on their property was the last thing the couple heard before drifting off into a peaceful sleep for the night. Wendy and Jason woke in the early morning to the sound of King barking incessantly. Jason pulled himself out of bed to see what King was fussing about. As he walked downstairs, a loud knock on the door greeted Jason.

Startled, Jason asked who was on the other side of the door. A man, obviously in distress, answered, saying he needed help. Jason opened the door, to a man slumped over on the porch, whose clothing was torn and dirty. Realizing the man was injured, Jason helped him into the house. He called Wendy to come help, as he settled the injured man into a kitchen chair.

Wendy came down from the bedroom, immediately putting a kettle of water on the wood stove to boil. She knew the man's wounds would need to be cleaned at once to stave off the chance of infection. The man said his name was Rex and he had been mauled by a bear while out hunting. Yesterday, in the late afternoon, after an unsuccessful hunting trip for deer, he was on his way home to Dawson when he surprised a mother bear and her two cubs. The bear attacked without warning, knocking him to the ground, slashing him in two places with her claws. Rex said he played dead, laying as still as possible and not even breathing. The bear, sensing Rex was no longer a threat, discontinued the attack and left the area with her cubs.

Unfortunately for Rex, when the bear charged, he hurt his ankle as he fell and now could not walk. He had crawled through the forest all night, gun in hand, until he came upon Wendy and Jason's house. Not able to travel any further, he knocked on the couple's door for help. Wendy cleaned Rex's wounds, which fortunately were not serious. Rex was a lucky man, escaping with his life from this dangerous encounter with an apex predator. The Yukon granted Rex another chance at life, something which does not happen often when careless hunters encountered bears in this savage land.

CHAPTER SEVENTEEN

Once he was bandaged and had some coffee, Rex was anxious to get home. Jason told Wendy he would retrieve Omar from the barn, letting Rex ride the donkey into town. Rex told Wendy his wife would be beside herself with worry, as he had failed to return home yesterday from his hunting trip. When a man goes hunting alone in the Yukon and does not come home by nightfall, the chances of seeing him alive again were slim to none.

Jason walked to the barn and led the donkey to the house, where Rex was waiting. Jason and Wendy helped place Rex onto Omar's back. Holding the reins, Jason led the donkey the short distance to Dawson. After a brief walk through town, Rex pointed out his home to Jason. Upon arrival, the entourage was met by barking dogs and a crying wife, who thought she would never see her husband again. With Jason's assistance, Rex disembarked from Omar and was helped into the house by his wife and Jason. Upon leaving, Jason was thanked many times by the appreciative couple, who found themselves together again, not always a given in this land called the Yukon.

Jason decided since he was already in town, he would

walk over to the site of Samuel's new ironware store. Upon seeing Jason and Omar, Samuel walked to meet them, his hands outstretched in greeting. He instantly fell in love with Omar, telling Jason he had owned donkeys in his past. He knew if these animals were treated right, they would become loyal friends and sometimes your protector. Omar was already that animal, basking in the spoils of life few of his brethren would ever partake in.

Samuel asked Jason if Omar was available for hire. He explained he periodically needed a pack animal at the build site for jobs requiring an animal with a strong back. He had been renting one from the livery stable, however, the one he had been using was uncooperative, and difficult to work with. Jason agreed to let Samuel use Omar on occasion, until the construction of the store was completed.

Jason told Samuel, he and Wendy had decided to go to Skagway for him, the couple accepting his job offer. Jason told him some logistical problems needed to be solved, but he was confident these issues could be worked out. This would allow the couple to travel later this summer, a trip Wendy and Jason were now looking forward to.

Arriving back home, Jason was surprised Jacob had stopped by to pick up Steward and Blossom's goods. Wendy said Jacob was using two pack animals to move the purchases to their cabin, a two day walk through a predator-filled forest. Jacob would have to sleep with one eye open and rifle in hand, as the scent from the mules would attract a lot of unwanted attention. Jacob had packed the mules and left town before Jason returned home from Dawson.

After lunch, the couple worked outside weeding the

vegetable garden and flowerbeds. Wendy and Jason were trying to keep the weeds from taking over the gardens. If left to grow unchecked, the weeds would lower the yield of vegetables and hide the beauty of the flowers. After pulling weeds for two hours, the couple decided they had done enough for the day. They returned to their house, lying down to enjoy an afternoon nap together, on a beautiful Yukon day.

CHAPTER EIGHTEEN

Wendy woke to the light pattering of raindrops on the roof. A cool breeze blew through the open windows of the bedroom. She pulled herself from the comfort of the bed, leaving Jason to nap longer. With money Jason had made working for Samuel, she had bought a nice piece of beef from one of the last riverboats to bring fresh food up the river to Dawson. The warming climate would stop deliveries of meat until the weather cooled again in the fall. Tonight, Wendy planned on cooking Jason a roast beef dinner. She had bought enough meat to also make a stew tomorrow. Along with King, the couple's dog, there should not be an issue eating this food before it spoiled.

The late afternoon was calm, the sky darkening as nighttime approached. The faint light from the twinkling stars could be seen in the dusky sky, along with the light from the full moon. Jason had awakened to the smell of roast beef cooking. His stomach growled with anticipation, as he thought about eating dinner. His senses picked up the aroma of fresh baked bread, intermingled with the delicious smell of the roast beef.

Jason joined Wendy in the kitchen, telling her how

delicious her cooking smelled. She told him dinner would be a bit longer, so he went outside to feed the sled dogs. He had been buying fresh fish from an Indigenous couple who lived in Dawson. They netted fish from a tributary of the Yukon River, selling their catch to those who needed to feed their hungry dogs in town. It was a lucrative business, which earned the couple a good income.

Returning to the house, Wendy announced dinner was ready. The roast beef was succulent, along with the potatoes and carrots she had cooked with the meat. The beef eaten with the fresh bread was a meal rarely served in the Yukon. Everyone, including Kuzih, enjoyed dinner, the beef being a special treat. The small family spent the remainder of the evening in the living room, Kuzih playing with a set of blocks while his parents read.

The following morning, while lying awake in bed, Jason became curious about the access panel in the ceiling of the bedroom. Since moving into this house, Wendy and Jason had never explored the attic. There was an opening in the ceiling, fitted with a wooden cover, which could be pushed up and onto the floor of the attic. Wendy and Jason had shown no interest in investigating this part of the house, making Jason wonder what was up there.

After breakfast, Jason, out of curiosity, pulled the tall dresser underneath the attic access. Standing on top of the dresser, he pushed the cover off and pulled himself up into the uppermost floor of the house. Wendy and Kuzih watched, and when he said it was safe, they decided to follow him up. Wendy lifted their son to Jason and then, standing on the dresser, let Jason pull her up into the attic with him.

The couple looked around, letting their eyes adjust to the low light streaming in through the small window situated at the far end of the room. Strewn about the floor were items from Bev's past. An old sled, Bev's father had made when she was a child, was their most valuable find, a personal heirloom no amount of money could buy. There were several wooden boxes and crates, including some holding Christmas decorations and one filled with trinkets from Bev's childhood. Many things had been stored away and forgotten about in this secret room no one ever talked about. Jason and Wendy let Kuzih pick one item to take with him and then gave up their search in the attic. They planned to come back another day and watch Bev's personal life unfold in front of them.

CHAPTER NINETEEN

Wendy and Jason awoke with sunshine streaming in through their bedroom windows. The couple was expecting company today, White Dove and Black Hawk, along with their dog, Nicky, were to arrive at their home in Dawson. From here, Jason was planning on escorting the young couple to Johnathan and Shining Star's cabin, a two day walk from this location. Johnathan and Shining Star would then travel with White Dove and Black Hawk to their new home, a three hour walk on a well-travelled trail. Unfortunately, Wendy would need to stay home and care for the animals, while her husband was away.

Shortly after lunch, King's barking announced the young couple's arrival. They were greeted warmly by Wendy and Jason and ushered into the house. Nicky chose to stay outside with King to get acquainted and try to build a new friendship. King was looking at this young dog with love in his eyes, an emotion not shared at this time by the female husky.

As Jason explained the cabin in the bush was a two-day walk, with a stopover at a scenic lake located at the halfway point, Wendy invited White Dove and Black Hawk to spend the night. Already tired from their travels to town, the couple quickly agreed to this proposal. Jason told their company they would be eating lake trout for dinner, as he and Wendy had taken the canoe out earlier in the morning and caught enough fish to feed everyone, including his always hungry dogs. They would cook the succulent trout over the hot coals of a campfire this evening.

The two couples spent the afternoon socializing together. Jason and Wendy learned that, like Grey Wolf and Rose, they were being gifted a small dog team, a sled, and supplies needed for the winter season from their fathers. This promised gift would be delivered as soon as dogsled season began, once the lakes had frozen over. White Dove mentioned to Wendy that eventually they would like to breed Nicky, raising her puppies and training them as sled dogs.

The afternoon sun soon sank below the horizon, turning the day into night. Jason lit the fire, letting Kuzih, his four-year-old son, help him add kindling to the flames, making the fire grow. After a short while, the fire was sending a large column of smoke drifting into the forest. Jason cooked the fresh fish, the sweet smell of the meat attracting a hungry fox, who would wait patiently for any spoils left from dinner. King and Nicky lay quietly by the campfire, having bonded in a friendship King hoped would last for life.

The couples, along with their pets, enjoyed dinner together. Jason cooked the fish to perfection, the tender meat falling off the bones. Unfortunately for the waiting fox, all he found when he searched the grounds after the people had moved indoors, were fish bones. The canine moved on hungry, disappointed his long wait had been for nothing.

The night was black, the heavy cloud cover obscuring the stars in the sky. Silence had settled over the forest, as a hungry bear made a visit to where Jason had served the cooked fish. King and Nicky, sleeping by the woodstove, caught the scent of this feared enemy, lifting their heads, waiting, and listening. The bear, finding nothing of interest, continued to his next stop, where he hoped his luck would be better.

CHAPTER TWENTY

The morning dawned sunny and warm. White Dove and Black Hawk rolled over and sat up in bed. King and Nicky were by the front door of the house barking, wanting to be let outside. Black Hawk told his wife he was going downstairs to take care of the dogs and he would return to her shortly. Upon Black Hawk's return, the couple talked about the new life they were about to embark on. They hoped the forest community they would join would teach them about living in a wilderness cabin, alone in the bush. Survival in the Yukon meant watching out for one another and assisting your fellow man when they found themselves in trouble and in need of help.

After drifting back to sleep, the couple were awakened by Wendy, yelling upstairs that breakfast would be served in fifteen minutes. The young couple pulled themselves out from under the warm blankets on the bed and washed up, using the bowl and pitcher of water which had been left on the wash stand, gracing the bedroom wall. They then quickly got dressed, ready to start their day.

White Dove and Black Hawk were greeted warmly by Wendy and Jason as they entered the kitchen. Wendy explained Jason would take them to the previous owners of the vacant cabin they were moving into. It was a two day walk through the forest, with one night spent camping during the trip. After arriving at this destination, Jonathan and Shining Star, with their son, Grey Eagle, would take the couple on the three hour walk to their new cabin. Wendy would stay home to care for the animals and King would stay with her. Dogs acted as an early warning system, letting their owners know if an unseen danger was lurking nearby.

The departing group finished their breakfast and prepared to leave. Wendy kissed Jason goodbye, telling him to be safe and return to her the way he left her. She hugged White Dove and Black Hawk tightly, wishing them luck on this new endeavour they had chosen to undertake. King was not a happy dog, his girlfriend, Nicky, left, and he was not invited to go along with her. He might never see his beautiful canine again. King lay by the cold woodstove, his already lonely heart feeling the same. Wendy came and cuddled King, reassuring him he would see Nicky again.

It was a beautiful day in the Yukon. The blue sky shone with a brilliance only seen in the far north. Small cumulus clouds floated lazily across the sky. White Dove pointed out one of the clouds which resembled an angel. She took this as a sign from the gods, the new life the couple were embarking on would be a success.

The trio walked all day, stopping only briefly for lunch. In the late afternoon they reached the lake, which was the halfway point to their destination. Their walk tomorrow would not be as long or arduous, as the trail for the rest of their journey to Jonathan and Shining Star's cabin was relatively flat. The trio would camp here for the night and continue their journey in the morning.

CHAPTER TWENTY-ONE

The placid, blue waters of the lake shone like a diamond in the setting sun. Jason showed the couple where he usually camped, when staying at this wilderness outpost. The site was on a higher piece of ground, overlooking the water. Waterfowl could be seen flying low over the lake, trying to find a safe area to spend the night.

Black Hawk disappeared, saying he would return shortly. Thirty minutes later, he returned, carrying a dozen freshwater clams he had harvested from the lake. Jason was surprised at Black Hawk's ability to find these hidden treasures buried in the sand. He would cook the shellfish over the campfire tonight, the hungry campers eating them with the smoked fish Wendy had packed for the group to have for dinner.

Jason gathered some wood from the surrounding forest. The sun was setting below the horizon when Jason lit the campfire. The dry wood lit up the night, as the fire grew larger. The forest was quiet, like when a predator is stalking prey. Nicky raised her head in worry; when she looked toward the forest, she saw two beady red eyes staring back at her. She whined a warning to Black Hawk. Jason and Black Hawk scanned the forest around them but saw nothing unusual. The men would keep their rifles close at hand, until they felt whatever danger the dog perceived had passed.

The night was dark and quiet. The occasional call from a duck or other bird staying on the lake was the only sound to break the silence of the evening. Black Hawk roasted the fresh clams over the campfire. When opening the shell, the meat was succulent and tasted delicious. Eating the clams with the smoked lake trout created a scrumptious campfire dinner, enjoyed on a beautiful Yukon night. The flames burned low in the fire, as the last of the embers burned to ash. The weary travellers decided to lay their heads down and go to sleep.

The stillness of the night was soon disturbed by the snoring individuals sleeping on the ground. This noise, which echoed through the wilderness, was keeping an annoyed Nicky, who was trying to get some sleep, awake. The dog thought, sometimes humans could be so irritating.

The bright sun was peeking over the treeline at the end of the expansive lake. Jason had awoken White Dove and Black Hawk to watch the sunrise, knowing what a beautiful sight it was to behold in the early morning sky. Having no food to eat, the trio packed up their belongings and continued their journey.

The day passed quickly, and near mid-afternoon the trio could hear dogs barking. Johnathan's huskies had picked up Nicky's scent. Johnathan and Shining Star were standing in the doorway of their cabin when the group arrived. A warm welcome was extended to the visitors, an extra greeting given

After the Gold Rush 59

to their newest neighbors, who would soon be living in their old cabin in the forest. Accepting a warm invitation to spend the night, Jason would leave for home in the morning. Black Hawk and White Dove would be taken to their cabin in the forest, where the couple's new life would begin.

CHAPTER TWENTY-TWO

The full moon shone its light down from the heavens, illuminating the forest and Johnathan's cabin which sat within it. Jason was awake, waiting for the first light of dawn. His back was sore from laying on the hard cabin floor all night. He had slept little and was looking forward to returning home and sleeping in his own bed. The first hint of daylight streamed through the windows of Johnathan and Shining Star's home. The full moon would retreat into the light of the morning sun, but would return to its former glory this evening, once more lighting the forest and cabin.

Jason pulled himself off the floor, sat on the chair, and put on his boots. The other people sleeping, upon hearing Jason awake, rose from their beds. Jason needed to stretch his legs, deciding to go for a short walk before returning to say goodbye and good luck to his friends. Jason walked over to where Jonathan kept his sled dogs. The huskies were glad to see him but were disappointed when he did not feed them. Next, he walked to the shoreline, where the morning light was bringing life back to the lake. Young waterfowl, of a variety of species, accompanied their parents in a search for food in the early light. Raptors flew overhead, looking for an easy meal, while the slap of a beaver's tail on the quiet lake could not be ignored.

Jason returned to his old cabin, thinking what a beautiful location their old homestead had been built on. After having coffee with his friends and family, he wished them good luck, hugging each one tightly before leaving on his long walk back to Dawson. Johnathan and Shining Star's cabin grew quiet after Jason left. Shining Star was packing a few things to take on their walk with Black Hawk and White Dove. Grey Eagle would be accompanying his parents, the young boy's legs having grown strong from the many lengthy walks he had taken throughout his short life.

Food in the Yukon this time of year was scarce. Waterfowl and fish from the lake were readily available during the summer, as well as small game, such as rabbits and grouse. However, the latter two were more difficult to secure, and not a reliable food source. No refrigeration meant a short shelf life for meat, which had to be eaten within a short time of being harvested. Eating bad meat had led to the deaths of many hungry trappers living in the bush.

Johnathan secured the cabin door, and the group were on their way. The trail they would walk to Black Hawk and White Dove's cabin was clearly marked. The day was sunny and warm, and the walk was pleasant and uneventful. Johnathan shot two fat squirrels and a rabbit while on the trail, ensuring food for dinner. Nicky sensed something different about the trail, running ahead and finding her future home with Black Hawk and White Dove. Nicky barked with excitement, wanting the group to see what she had found, a cabin situated in a beautiful wilderness setting. Alone in a forest no more, life would return to the cabin, providing safety and comfort to this couple who would call this special place home.

CHAPTER TWENTY-THREE

Johnathan opened the cabin door, allowing Black Hawk and White Dove to enter the structure. He had performed regular maintenance on the building while it had sat dormant for over a year. The cabin and outbuildings were in pristine condition, with the house move-in ready. Johnathan continued to show the couple their new property, including the nearby lake. He pointed out the canoe and paddles, which came with the cabin. He showed Black Hawk the fur shed, which was fully equipped for fur trapping. Johnathan had left all his traps behind when the couple moved into Jason and Wendy's cabin. As Jason was not trapping in Dawson, he had left his traps behind for Johnathan. Shining Star took White Dove out to see where the garden had been located, as well as showing her the outdoor freezer.

After Johnathan and Shining Star were confident they had explained the workings of the cabin, they felt it was time to leave. The couples hugged one another goodbye, with the previous cabin owners wishing the new residents good luck on their new start in life. Shining Star offered her and Johnathan's help in any way if it was needed. Johnathan told the couple to feel free to stop in to visit whenever they wanted.

With those last words, Johnathan, Shining Star, and Grey Eagle headed toward home. Nicky was enjoying her new surroundings, the dog busy investigating and mapping out the territory around her new home and surrounding forest. Black Hawk and White Dove walked to the lake, where they gazed across the water at the distant shore. The lake was calm, except for a slight ripple across the surface. After gazing at the placid blue water, the couple's unsure spirits were calmed by its beauty and the innocence it represented.

Black Hawk and White Dove turned around, directing their attention back to the cabin. Johnathan had given the game he had shot on the journey here to the couple, which needed to be cleaned and readied for cooking. Black Hawk headed to the fur shed while White Dove went in the house to light the stove. Before long, puffs of grey were coming from the cabin chimney, drifting lazily in the wind through the surrounding forest. After cleaning the small game, Black Hawk fed the remains of the animals to Nicky. Whatever the dog did not eat, he would dispose of in the forest, for the scavengers to take care of. He took the meat inside for White Dove to cook on the woodstove.

It had been a beautiful day in the Yukon, clear blue skies and warm air dominating the first day at the couple's new home. After eating dinner, a feeling of peace and comfort overwhelmed the couple as they sat around the campfire with their young husky, Nicky. The call of the Yukon had taken hold of these adventurers and an everlasting commitment to this wilderness would prevail. Nature would give the couple an honest chance at survival but would not guarantee their life in this harsh but beautiful land.

CHAPTER TWENTY-FOUR

After a tiring two day walk through the forest, Jason finally reached Dawson. Wendy and his son, Kuzih, welcomed him home with open arms. The couple did not like to be separated, not even for a short amount of time. King was looking for attention from Jason, as he had not seen him in a few days and had missed his presence around the house.

After resting for a short while, Jason took King to the lake, throwing sticks in the water for the dog to retrieve. They returned to the house after playing this game for thirty minutes, King's need for attention satisfied. Wendy was preparing something for Jason to eat, as the only thing he had consumed during his journey home were berries he had found along the trail. Happy to be home, Jason spent the rest of the day with his small family, sleeping soundly through the night, tired from his trip.

The following morning, Wendy, Jason, and Kuzih decided to take a walk into Dawson to pick up coffee, sugar, and flour. While in town, they went to see how construction was going on Samuel's new ironware store. Kuzih was very interested in watching the men work on the new building.

The job had been moving along smoothly, with the tentative completion date now expected to be in mid-July. Samuel said the work crew was four weeks ahead of schedule and told Wendy and Jason they should plan on taking their trip to Alaska soon.

Sam told the couple he would like for them to leave for Skagway in approximately four weeks, which would allow for the building to be completed and ready to be stocked with goods immediately upon their return. Although the couple knew they would miss their son while gone, they were beginning to look forward to their trip.

Before they began to walk back home, Samuel asked Jason if he and Omar were available to spend two days working for him, starting tomorrow. Jason told him they were both free and he would be at the job site by 8 a.m.. With their business done, Jason and his family headed toward home, to find King waiting at the front door wanting to be let inside. Wendy opened the door, and she followed King into the house. Jason went to feed his dog team and the animals residing in the barn, with Kuzih tagging along.

Thirty minutes later, Jason and his son returned from their chores, to find Wendy had the fire going and the kettle boiling. The couple sat down for coffee and to discuss their upcoming trip to Alaska. Samuel was planning for their transportation to and from Skagway. He had told them they should expect to know the details of their travel plans within two weeks. They were both slightly apprehensive of the journey. Jason decided to take King and their son for a walk around the lake. The day had turned sunny and warm, the lake's calm water sparkled in the bright sunshine. Squirrels, sensing King's presence, chattered noisily from the treetops as the group of hikers walked by. A young deer bolted in front of them, having been grazing on the green grass which grew in abundance along the path. Upon seeing King, the deer bounded into the forest with the dog in hot pursuit. Kuzih laughed at the series of events unfolding in front of him, the deer leaping away and King barking as he ran. The dog soon returned, panting and out of breath, with his tail wagging. This carefree attitude is not enjoyed often in the Yukon, where survival takes precedence over enjoyment.

CHAPTER TWENTY-FIVE

Shortly after returning home from their walk around the lake, there was a knock on the front door. Jason went to answer, wondering who this unexpected visitor could be. He yelled in a loud voice for the person on the other side of the door to identify themselves. A dog's welcoming bark was the first reply, Jason instantly recognizing Rusty's bark. He opened the door to a smiling Joe and Mary standing in the doorway. Rusty barged right past Jason into the house, impatient to see his friend King. Jason graciously invited Joe and Mary inside and Wendy placed a kettle of water on the stove to make coffee.

Mary explained to Wendy they had walked to Dawson to buy sewing supplies, as she needed to make a new fishing net and repair holes in the other two she owned. Joe needed to pick up ammunition for his rifle, as he always kept an extra two boxes on hand at the cabin. Running out of these precious cartridges could result in no way to protect oneself from a large predator and limited one's ability to find food. Coffee, sugar, and flour, not always available in Dawson, were also on their shopping list.

Wendy and Jason invited the couple to stay for dinner and sleep overnight in a warm comfortable bed upstairs. It was an invitation Joe and Mary would never refuse. Leaving Rusty with Wendy and Jason, the couple walked into town to do their shopping. They returned two hours later, carrying all the goods they had been searching for.

Mary and Wendy went outdoors to finish weeding the garden, in preparation of planting it. The growing season is short in the Yukon, but a good gardener can harvest excellent crops from the rich soil. Early June was just around the corner and the time to plant the garden would soon be here. Wendy and Mary wore hats from Bev's large selection she had left to Wendy when she died. The day was sunny and hot, and the hats the women wore kept them cool.

When Wendy and Jason were in town earlier, they had purchased some fresh meat for dinner. With potatoes and carrots, they had secured at the general store, Wendy was planning to prepare venison stew for dinner. She would bake bread in the oven of the woodstove to complement her delicious stew.

The men said goodbye to the happy donkeys in the barn and returned to the house. While the women worked in the garden, the men had cleaned the donkey pens. Omar, Honey, and Baby Jack were happy to get fresh bedding and a treat. Jason had stopped by the livery stable while in town and bought some of the special mash the owner made up especially for donkeys. When the animals knew this food was their reward for working hard, they put in extra effort while on the job. The proprietor of the stable was always quick to brag to Jason he had finally figured out how to make lazy donkeys work hard. This was a bold statement, which Omar and his family would not like to hear.

CHAPTER TWENTY-SIX

The hungry dinner party sat around Wendy's kitchen table. In front of the guests sat a pot of venison stew, its delicious odor tantalizing the appetites of the men and women ready to eat. The two dogs, King, and Rusty, were also waiting, having strategically taken up begging positions by the table. After serving everyone dinner, Wendy and Jason confirmed their plans to travel to Skagway for Samuel. Joe and Mary were surprised to hear of this change of events but were happy to stay in Dawson for an extended period of time. Jason told the couple, unless they heard otherwise, they should plan to arrive for their housesitting and childcare duties in four weeks.

After dinner, the two couple's retired to the living room, where they played euchre, a popular card game, until their tired eyes could take no more. The group laughed at King and Rusty, who were snoring loudly, asleep by the fireplace. The couples retired to their respective bedrooms, wishing each other a good night and a restful sleep. Joe and Mary undressed and crawled under the blankets of the very comfortable bed located in their room. Within minutes, they were sleeping soundly. The quiet of the night which surrounded them, sent the couple into an undisturbed sleep until dawn the following morning.

Jason was awake early. He wanted to eat a light breakfast before heading to the barn to feed the donkeys and prepare Omar to work at Samuel's construction site today. Joe and Mary were leaving after breakfast, to go back to their cabin with their loyal dog Rusty. The couple would return to Dawson in about a month to look after Wendy and Jason's property. Joe and Mary's responsibilities would also include looking after their child, Kuzih, and the animals living with them. Wendy and Jason would be gone for up to two weeks, unable to give a firm date as to when they would return.

Jason left the house early with Omar. He arrived at the construction site, using the donkey to move a pile of rocks, leftover from when the men dug the basement. A large double canvas bag was placed across Omar's back, and each bag was filled with an equal number of stones. Omar then transported the cargo to a neighboring lot, where the owner wanted to build a wall out of them. As the day wore on Omar, was in agony. His back hurt so badly, he finally sat on the ground refusing to move.

Understanding Omar's pain, Jason removed the bags from the donkey's back and led him to a grassy area where he could eat and relax. Jason decided then to take Omar back home to his wife and child, who were waiting for him in the barn. He found Sam and told him he was leaving work early due to Omar's sore back and feelings of exhaustion. To Omar, this was the hardest day ever in the history of him working as a pack animal.

Jason told Samuel, Omar had put in a good day's work,

but he did not think it wise to continue using his small pack animal for transporting such heavy loads. Samuel agreed, saying he would rent a larger pack animal from the livery stable to finish moving the rock. Omar was elated to be going home, and wondered if Jason realized he was old, and his back was too weak for moving heavy stones. Omar was afraid he could be crippled for life if he continued to do this heavy work. Jason took a hobbling and thankful Omar home, where the donkey wished to be. Omar's wife would nurse him back to health and the donkey hoped he would never have to repeat this dreadful experience again.

CHAPTER TWENTY-SEVEN

Jason and Omar returned from the construction site around 3 p.m.. He led Omar to his pen and fed and watered the donkeys and chickens before returning to the house. Upon seeing Jason, Wendy asked if Omar was hurt on the job today, as she had noticed him struggling to walk when Jason led him to the barn. Jason explained to Wendy about the heavy rock their donkey carried on his back. He told her Omar was so tired and sore he laid down and refused to stand back up, which was why they were home early from work. Wendy assured Jason Omar's back would heal after resting for a time.

As it was still early, the couple decided to take the canoe out on the lake. The air was warm, and the wind was calm, making it a perfect day to go canoeing. Jason was hoping Wendy would be able to catch enough fish to feed themselves and their dogs for dinner tonight with her net. They launched the canoe in the bright sunshine and clear blue sky, the craft sliding, like a sled on ice, across the glassy surface of the water. The couple, along with Kuzih who was seated in the middle of the boat, paddled the canoe along the shoreline looking for wildlife to watch. They were rewarded by seeing a bull moose eating in a marshy area along the shoreline. His rack of antlers made him the tallest and most formidable mammal living in the bush. Weighing up to a fifteen hundred pounds, a bull moose is one animal no one would want to step on them, if encountered in the forest.

Wendy and Jason continued paddling across the tranquil water of the lake. Waterfowl filled the air, the lake being a prime breeding ground for many species of these birds. Jason chose to only shoot these animals when no other food source was available, as he hated plucking them, a time consuming and difficult task.

Soon, they reached the area where Wendy would use her nets to hopefully catch whitefish and lake trout. One hour later, the bottom of the canoe was full of fish. The couple left the area with enough food to feed themselves and their pack of hungry huskies. Upon their return home, King met the couple at the shoreline. Jason threw his dog the smallest whitefish in the boat, knowing King was hungry and had not eaten anything except what he had been able to catch for himself. King was not a good hunter, being untrained in the art of fending for himself.

The couple carried the fish toward home, taking them to the large outdoor shed where Jason would clean them. But before doing so, they washed up and decided to lay down for a nap with Kuzih. When they woke, they would begin working on the chores which needed to be done before dinner. King, after eating his whitefish, had the same idea, also laying down inside.

A wolverine lurking out back was waiting for an opportunity to steal dinner, hopefully from an unlocked shed. With luck, it had been left open by a careless ex-fur trapper who had obviously not learned his lesson, after having this same thing happen to him twice while living in the forest. If Jason was lucky, the hungry wolverine might leave him a fish or two for dinner.

CHAPTER TWENTY-EIGHT

The wolverine waited for his moment, the opportunity to steal Jason and Wendy's fish from the shed. After hearing and sensing no movement coming from or around the house, the wolverine made his move, stealthily moving closer toward his objective. Unfortunately for the wolverine, the shed was locked. The animal's hopes for an easy meal were dashed by a man who had learned his lesson the last time he had been outwitted in this fashion. Jason foiled the plans of this cunning enemy whom he shared the forest with. The wolverine slinked back into the woods, discouraged at the result of what he thought would be an easy opportunity to secure a meal.

Wendy and Jason awoke from their nap. King stirred, changing his position on the floor, and fell back into a peaceful sleep. Jason pulled himself from the bed, telling Wendy he was going to the shed to clean the lake trout for dinner. He woke King on his way out the door, encouraging the dog to come with him. Jason started the smoker, planning to cook some of the fish this way. He would also fillet some of the trout for Wendy to cook inside on the woodstove, planning to eat the fish with his wife and son around a campfire later this evening.

Initially staying with Jason, King left when he realized he was not going be fed until dinner. The dog decided to explore the forest, heading off on the trail which surrounded the lake. Jason continued cleaning the large number of trout the couple had caught earlier in the day. With his work finished, Jason noticed his dog had not returned from wherever he had ventured off to. Jason had a hunch King was in trouble and decided to go look for him.

Jason began his search by walking on the trail he and Wendy had been clearing, following the shoreline of the lake. Jason called King's name but got no response. Soon, a rancid odor caught Jason's attention. A skunk had sprayed something, and Jason hoped it was not his dog. Shortly after noticing this foul odor, Jason heard the muffled sound of a whining dog. Exploring the source of this noise in the otherwise quiet forest, he found King with his upper body squeezed into a hollow stump. The skunk he had been chasing had run into the log to escape from the dog. King, with no regard for the consequences of his actions, dove headfirst into the opening, trapping himself. The skunk, feeling threatened, let off his protective shield, almost smothering King, who was trapped in this unsavory predicament. The skunk had calmy exited the hollow stump from the other end and continued on his way.

Jason advanced slowly towards his smelly dog. He briefly thought about leaving this stinking mess, going home to think about what he should do. Suddenly, and without much thought, Jason sprang into action. He grabbed King's rear end and pulled him hard, releasing him from his prison. King held his head in shame, knowing he would be sleeping outside with the sled dogs until he smelled better. This was not something pleasant for a spoiled canine to have to live with, in a land which offers no outside comforts to a domesticated dog.

CHAPTER TWENTY-NINE

Jason walked home, making King keep a distance between them. After telling Wendy what happened, the couple both laughed at what their dog had gotten himself into. Wendy told Jason she knew of a plant her mother had used as an antidote to the skunk smell. She asked Jason to start a large fire outside in the firepit to boil water in their large cast iron pot. While he did this, she collected the plant they needed from the forest. Returning home, she boiled the leaves and stalks in the water, creating a witches' brew, a dark brown liquid, which was left to cool.

This mysterious plant, when mixed with water, created a prescription which neutralizes the smell of the skunk, leaving the dog smelling normal. After being bathed in this concoction, King was saved, once again allowed to sleep in his favorite spot by the fireplace. He did not have to spend the nights alone, left outside in the dark. Did King learn a lesson from this ordeal he created for himself? Probably not.

The trout Jason had placed in the smoker was finished cooking. He removed the fish from the heat and placed it on a platter to cool, carrying it into the cabin for safekeeping, until they were ready to eat. After taking care of King's issue,

Jason let the campfire burn down, resulting in a smaller flame coming from the burning wood. This created a more intimate atmosphere for sitting and eating around the fire.

Before the day turned to night, Wendy and Jason took a walk to the lake. The couple sat by the shore with their son, Wendy's head laying on Jason's lap as they watched the sun sink below the horizon. The couple felt alone, but they were not lonely. The beauty of the Yukon encompassing the twosome, coupled with the love they felt for each other and their son, made them happy with the life they chose.

Wendy and Jason returned to the house with Kuzih, retrieved the fish, and took it outside by the fire. The sky was dark, with only the twinkling stars lighting the land below. The family sat quietly around the campfire, eating the fish Jason had smoked earlier. King ate his fill of the succulent fillets, which he had learned to enjoy more than eating the fish raw. The soulful call of the loon echoed from the quiet lake, the lonely male bird looking for his lost mate.

After dinner, Wendy took her son inside to put to bed, leaving Jason and King to enjoy the fire a bit longer. Jason reached for King, pulling him close. The dog snuggled against Jason's neck, showering his face with wet, slippery kisses. Living in this land, a trust and inseparable bond had developed between the man and his dog, as they depended on each other for their survival in this unforgiving place, called the Yukon.

CHAPTER THIRTY

Jason woke to an early morning knock on the front door of his house. He told Wendy to stay in bed while he went downstairs to see who their visitor was. When Jason arrived downstairs, King was already waiting at the front door, with his tail wagging. He also wondered who this visitor might be. Jason yelled at the stranger to identify themselves. The man on the other side of the door told Jason he was a constable stationed at the North West Mounted Police office in Dawson. Jason opened the door and invited the man inside the house.

The man identified himself as Winslow, a recent immigrant to Canada from England. Winslow had been a police officer in London, when his father had travelled from England to Canada to participate in the gold rush which plagued the Yukon during the late nineteenth century. Unfortunately, his father died, buried under twenty feet of snow, during an avalanche on his way to the Klondike. Winslow's desire to follow his father's footsteps to this remote place was a mission he could not fully explain, but something he felt he must do. He told Jason he had worked in Edmonton as a constable for the North West Mounted

Police stationed there. When an opening arose in this most northern detachment, he applied and was offered the transfer, to a place he felt he belonged.

Winslow then went on to explain to Jason why he was here. Last night, a stranger in town had shot two unarmed men dead, after a disagreement in a bar in Dawson. The man was seen leaving the area, heading out of town, toward the trails which would take him deep in the bush. The detachment was looking for experienced men, educated in the ways of nature, to join a search party for this desperate man. The posse was meeting at the detachment's headquarters, before beginning their search. Winslow asked Jason if he would help, which Jason agreed to do, as soon as he grabbed something to eat, dressed, and gathered up the supplies he needed. Winslow told Jason there was food for the volunteers being served at the station, thanked Jason, and left to return to headquarters.

Jason went upstairs and woke Wendy, who had slept through the entire conversation he had with Winslow. He told Wendy the story the constable had told him and how he had offered his help in looking for, and hopefully apprehending, this man hiding out in the forest. Jason dressed, gathered up a few personal belongings, such as his rifle, and kissed his wife good-bye. By the time Jason arrived at the police station, six other volunteers from Dawson were already there, preparing for their manhunt in the bush. After satisfying their hungry stomachs, the men, which included an Indigenous tracker, were divided into two-man teams. Each pair would search the various trails, looking for signs of recent activity of the desperate man. The volunteers, along with the constables, headed off in different directions, all hoping for the same result, the capture of a wanted killer, taken dead or alive.

CHAPTER THIRTY-ONE

The day was sunny and warm, as the men left the headquarters of the North West Mounted Police in Dawson. Jason had been paired with a man named Ruby, an experienced hunter and fur trapper who lived in town. Ruby suggested the man they were looking for did not have much of a chance of surviving in the harsh environment he chose to hide in. With only the clothes on his back and a pistol in his hand, the hunted could not survive long. The man's only chance for life would be to surrender and be taken back to Dawson to stand trial.

Jason and Ruby left the station, walking to the far end of town, before heading down a trail which led to a deserted mining shack. An old man had spent a summer here panning for gold in the creek which passed by his shelter. He had built the ramshackle hovel from the remnants of an old cabin he had discovered nearby. Unfortunately, before the fall of that year, the man had become another grim statistic of the Yukon, falling prey to thieves who were convinced he had discovered a large amount of gold. Accosted by these two men, he was shot and killed on his claim for fifty dollars worth of gold nuggets.

Ruby suggested they search this area first, as perhaps the killer had come this way. If the man found the prospector's old shack, he might stay there temporarily, before moving on to a different location. Jason and Ruby made their way into the forest, following the trail until they came upon a fast-flowing stream. Ruby led the way down the seldom used trail. After a thirty-minute walk, the shack they were looking for came into view, obscured in the trees ahead. Jason and Ruby cautiously approached the shack, although there did not appear to have been any recent activity in the area.

Suddenly a gunshot rang out, the bullet ricocheting off a large rock beside Ruby. The men retreated into the safety of the forest. Ruby yelled out to the man, informing him a heavily armed posse from Dawson was searching for him and to save his own life he needed to surrender. A heavy silence gripped the surrounding forest. Shortly thereafter, a gunshot rang out and then total silence again. The desperate man had taken his own life, rather than spend the rest of his natural life in prison. This tragedy was brought on by a wrong decision made during a drunken brawl over money.

The killer's body was taken back to Dawson and buried in the pauper's section of the Dawson cemetery. Even though he had shot himself, Jason and Ruby shared a one-hundred-dollar reward for the apprehension of the wanted man. The people in the town were happy this man no longer posed a threat to Dawson and the surrounding cabins located throughout the forest.

CHAPTER THIRTY-TWO

The month of June was well underway. Spring in the Yukon was beginning to blossom into summer. The green meadows, once void of colour, were now filled with wildflowers in full bloom. The summer season was taking hold, changing the landscape of this inhospitable land.

Jason had spent four days over the last two weeks working for Samuel, doing carpentry work on the inside of his new ironware store. Samuel told Jason he had made final preparations for their trip to Alaska and had a departure date for him. Jason told Samuel, he and his family were taking a trip into the bush, to visit someone at their cabin. However, they would return in plenty of time to prepare for their journey to oversee the transfer of his wares.

Wendy and Jason had been discussing a trip to visit Black Hawk and White Dove, the young Indigenous couple Wendy had gifted Johnathan and Shining Star's former cabin to. Wendy had promised they would come visit the couple in their new home before the snow came. Going to visit now, may be the only time they would be able to make the journey there before winter. Wendy had planned with a cousin, who lived in Dawson, to come daily to feed

After the Gold Rush 89

and water the animals living on their property. The couple planned on leaving early tomorrow morning for the long trek through the forest.

Jason picked up a supply of moose jerky from a man in Dawson who specialized in such products. This nonperishable food was nutritious and easy to carry when on expeditions into the bush. Jason bought some extra jerky as a gift for the young couple they were visiting. He also stopped by the livery stable and purchased a high-calorie dog food and some special mash for the donkeys.

The morning sun shone through the open windows of Wendy and Jason's bedroom. A warm breeze caressed the faces of the couple, awakening them from their peaceful sleep. The couple pulled themselves out of bed and walked downstairs to the kitchen. Jason let King outside, while Wendy went back upstairs to rouse their son, Kuzih, who was still sleeping. The couple grabbed some bread Wendy baked yesterday to eat while on the trail this morning. Both adults carried knapsacks on their backs with the few items needed for their trip.

Jason secured the door to the house and called King. The family left Dawson, walking toward the outskirts of town, where their journey would begin. Numerous trails led into the forest. Jason picked the path they would walk on for the two-day trip to their destination. The day was hot, the relentless sun beaming down on the travellers hiking the difficult terrain.

After walking for four hours, the tired party stopped for lunch and a rest. The group shared jerky together, except for King who ate the dry concoction of food made specifically for dogs by the creator of the special mash for the donkeys. The proprietor of the livery stable had thought up some ingenious ways to make money, keeping customers coming back for more of the same product. He believed to be a success in life, a man needs to come up with new ideas regularly. The success of which made him one of the wealthiest business owners in Dawson at this time, a title this man wore proudly.

CHAPTER THIRTY-THREE

The group of travellers enjoyed a sixty-minute rest before continuing their journey. After another four-hour walk, they would reach the lake where they planned to camp overnight. The relentless sun beat down on the hikers, making their walk to Black Hawk and White Dove's cabin even more difficult. The forest around them was quiet, with the occasional chatter of a squirrel high in the treetops the only sound to break the silence and serenity which engulfed them. The sound of distant thunder made the couple wonder if they were going to stay dry tonight.

The afternoon wore on and the group of weary travellers finally found themselves at their destination. The blue waters of the lake beckoned the sweaty humans to shed their clothing and jump into the cold water to cool off. Wendy took their son, Kuzih, placing him into the lake, letting him enjoy the feel of the refreshing water against his hot skin. King also got in on the action, jumping off the shore into the water numerous times. By the time the swimmers were done frolicking in the lake, the sun was setting. The small family returned to the area where they would be sleeping tonight.

Jason gathered wood and started a campfire, to

provide light during the dark Yukon night. The sky, filled with clouds, created a blackness in the forest, making it impossible to see what was in front of them. The darkness, combined with the quiet, made their night's sleep peaceful, the solitude causing everyone to sleep until sunrise, the following morning. Jason, believing it was going to be another hot day, wanted to start the second half of their journey at daybreak. The group met that goal, sharing some jerky for breakfast before gathering up their belongings and leaving the peaceful lakeside setting.

The day was hot, like yesterday, making the journey harder and longer. Finally, in the late afternoon, Black Hawk and White Dove's cabin came into view. Upon seeing the building, King ran ahead, barking loudly, announcing Wendy and Jason's presence. The young couple came to the door, surprised and happy to see company. White Dove invited the couple into their cabin. Nicky remembered her old friend, King, who she met while at Wendy and Jason's house in Dawson. The dogs wanted outside so they could play together; Black Hawk granting the dogs' wishes.

The cabin looked nice; White Dove having decorated the interior to the couple's taste with what they had to work with. She had made the cabin feel comfortable and inviting. Black Hawk told Jason they had been eating rabbit frequently for the last few weeks, as there was an unusually large population which seemed to not be diminishing, no matter how many were shot and eaten. Wendy laughed when White Dove told her rabbit was on the menu for dinner.

Black Hawk told Wendy and Jason they had been working on cutting enough firewood for the winter season.

The couple had cut and piled wood in the bush, expecting to retrieve it when Black Hawk's father brought their dog team. This would happen during the early months of winter, after the snows arrived. After the hosts and their company ate dinner, the couples spent the rest of the evening playing cards, till their eyes grew heavy and sleepy. Exhausted from their long walk through the bush, Wendy, Jason, and Kuzih's fatigue guaranteed them a peaceful night's sleep in the quiet forest.

CHAPTER THIRTY-FOUR

Nicky and King stirred in their sleep; the dogs had heard a noise outside the house. A bear roamed around the yard, stopping at the fire pit. The predator dug through the ashes of the campfire, trying to find the source of the smell which attracted him here. After finding nothing of interest, the bear lumbered off into the dark forest to continue his search for food. Hearing the bear leave, King and Nicky breathed a sigh of relief, laid their heads back down, and fell asleep for rest of the night.

The morning sun shone through the cabin windows, waking up the people sleeping inside. Wendy and Jason planned to leave Black Hawk and White Dove's cabin this morning for their long walk home. Black Hawk offered the leftovers from dinner last night to the departing couple and their son, which they gratefully accepted, knowing little food would be available to eat except from the occasional berry patch on the way home.

The families said their goodbyes, with Wendy extending an invitation for White Dove and Black Hawk to celebrate this Christmas at their house in Dawson. She explained about her Aunt Bev's tradition of celebrating the holiday with her relatives and adopted family who lived as fur trappers in the bush. Wendy told White Dove before Bev died, she made Wendy promise she would continue this act of kindness, which nature rarely provided to these people. Black Hawk told Wendy and Jason they hoped to see them at Christmas.

The couple turned, and with Kuzih and King, walked toward the trail home to Dawson. Late in the afternoon of the second day of travelling, Wendy and Jason sighted the familiar skyline of small homes which made up the growing city of Dawson. A short time later, the couple was home, entering their comfortable dwelling, glad to be finished with their trip into the forest.

Wendy lit the woodstove to boil some water for coffee. After enjoying some quiet time together, the couple talked about their upcoming journey to Skagway. Jason planned to go see Samuel in the morning, wanting to hear about the itinerary for their trip. Both he and Wendy were looking forward to the adventure and were glad Joe and Mary would be looking after things here at home.

The skies darkened, as a storm approached the area. Lightning lit up the approaching night, with heavy rain falling on the roof of the house. This caused a nervous King to cuddle into Jason, looking for safety from the storm. Jason hugged King tightly, comforting the dog as best he could. The storm passed, the sky cleared, and a million twinkling stars lit up the nighttime sky. A feeling of peace overcame this young family, a peace found only in the Yukon.

CHAPTER THIRTY-FIVE

A stiff breeze blew through the large trees which graced the front yard of Wendy and Jason's house. King was whining at the front door, waiting to be let outside to use the bathroom. Jason stirred, pulling himself out of bed. He walked downstairs to a dancing dog, who needed to be let outside. Jason opened the front door for King, allowing him to make his exit into the early morning dawn. Jason returned to his bedroom, joining his wife under the covers of their comfortable mattress.

An hour later, King's constant barking woke Jason. He pulled himself out of bed and walked to the window. One of Jason's sled dogs was loose, having escaped his restraints. Lucky for King, he was one of the only sled dogs that liked him. This dog would rather play with King, unlike the rest of the sled dogs who would prefer to fight with him. Jason dressed to go outside, needing to restrain the husky who had escaped his chain.

Finishing this task, Jason took a reluctant King back inside the house with him. Wendy was awake, making coffee, when Jason returned to the kitchen. Wendy had baked some bread in the woodstove's oven the previous evening and now served her husband a piece with jam for breakfast. After eating, Jason planned to visit Samuel, working for the day at his construction site and obtaining the updated information about their journey to Skagway.

The last time Jason spoke with Sam, he had asked if once Omar's back was strong again, he could return to complete some light duty work for him. Jason replied it was not a problem and would bring Omar with him today. Jason kissed Wendy goodbye and walked to the barn to retrieve Omar. The duo left for Dawson; Omar confident he would not be worked to exhaustion anymore.

The day was sunny and warm, and within ten minutes they were at the jobsite. The men were finishing the roof of the store, which would soon have a completed exterior. Samuel greeted Jason, shaking his hand, happy to see him. After handing Omar's reigns over to one of Samuel's workers, Jason joined Sam inside the new store. Jason looked around, admiring the fine construction work performed by the men Sam had hired.

Samuel told Jason he was working to complete the trip itinerary for him. He had a definitive departure date, as reservations had been made on the riverboat, which would take him and Wendy from Dawson down the Yukon to Whitehorse. From there they would travel by train, directly to the deep-water port in Skagway. The paddleboat departed Dawson weekly, and the tickets had been reserved to coincide with the arrival of the store's merchandise in Skagway.

Jason finished up the day, having almost completed the shelves and cabinets he had been working on. He retrieved Omar, who had relished in the attention the men he worked with today had given him. The donkey had been showered with treats and plenty of hugs during his workday but would be glad to return home to the comfort of his barn.

Jason and Omar walked home on this beautiful Yukon day, a man and his donkey returning after a good day's work. Omar was much happier returning from the job this time; having a vastly better work experience than when he thought he would be crippled for life. Such a debilitating injury would not have been good for a donkey in the Yukon. He had already escaped being used as bait to lure an annoying wolf pack or an aggressive bear to their deaths and was eternally thankful his back had healed. Omar was happy he was once again a productive animal, capable of earning his keep, living safely in the barn.

CHAPTER THIRTY-SIX

Samuel stopped by Wendy and Jason's home after he made all the final arrangements for the couple's trip. They were to board the riverboat a week from today at a dock in Dawson. The boat would travel down the Yukon River to Whitehorse, a four hundred mile journey. From Whitehorse, the couple would switch their mode of transportation to train. The train would take Wendy and Jason to Skagway in six hours, with multiple short stops at outposts built along the way. The train would drop supplies off at these desolate places and occasionally pick up passengers before leaving.

Wendy and Jason were to travel to the remote port of Skagway, where they would meet the ship carrying Samuel's goods for his new store. Samuel had purchased these items from the only foundry producing ironware on the west coast. Samuel's brother had checked on the quality of the goods he purchased in Portland and the accuracy of the manifest. Once this task was completed, the items had been loaded on a boat and sent to Skagway.

Over the next week, Wendy and Jason prepared for their trip. Joe and Mary arrived at Wendy and Jason's home two days before their departure date. They assured the couple they would take care of their son, Kuzih, and the family dog, King, while they were away. They would also be responsible for looking after the livestock and dog team, for the duration of Jason and Wendy's trip.

Yesterday, Jason had loaded the belongings they would need for the trip onto Omar. The luggage was taken to the docks and placed in a small room on the steamboat. Samuel had rented a cabin for the couple to sleep and rest in when they tired of standing on the boat's deck.

The following morning found John and Wendy hugging their son goodbye. Joe and Mary promised to look after King, who seemed to be as much responsibility as the child he played with. With one more hug for everyone, including the dog, Wendy and Jason left their house for town.

The boat they were boarding was waiting for them at the waterfront in Dawson. The couple walked to this location, boarding the steamship with plenty of time to spare. After a short while, the captain of the ship yelled, "All aboard!", and the paddle wheeler got ready to leave the dock. With one loud toot of its whistle, the boat departed for Whitehorse, heading down the mighty Yukon River.

People waved from the docks as the *Yukon Princess* left the dock where it had been moored. The boat's voyage would take it to Whitehorse, a four-hundred-mile journey. A wood-fired boiler would produce enough energy to power the paddle wheel, which propelled the boat forward. Wendy and Jason waved at the people who had gathered on the dock to watch the boat leave its moorings, its paddle churning loudly through the river water.

Jason and Wendy watched from the deck of the boat

as the city of Dawson disappeared into the background of virgin forest and fast flowing water, which surrounded the couple in every direction. Wendy wondered what her son was doing; she loved her little boy very much and already missed him. Wendy felt confident he was in good hands with Joe and Mary taking care of him.

CHAPTER THIRTY-SEVEN

Wendy and Jason stood on the deck of the *Yukon Princess*, watching the beauty of the wilderness forests flash before their eyes. Golden and bald eagles filled the northern sky, as they scanned the river for a quick meal of fish. Growing weary of standing at the rails, Jason and Wendy decided to go to their room. Samuel had reserved sleeping quarters for the couple. The room was small, with only a bed and a shelf occupying the space. With Jason and Wendy's belongings in the room, it felt like a closet, not a makeshift bedroom.

Lying on the bed, the gentle rocking of the boat soon caused the couple to fall into a peaceful sleep. Shortly after noon, the boat's whistle sounded. The Yukon Princess was stopping at a frontier town with a deep-water dock. This stop on the river was where the paddleboat would resupply their stock of firewood. Wood cut from the forests surrounding this boom town was needed to produce steam, which powered the giant wheel at the rear of the ship.

Jason and Wendy exited their stateroom. The dock was busy with people carrying goods on and off the boat. The captain introduced himself to Jason and Wendy as Barclay, their captain for the voyage to Whitehorse. He told the couple they could disembark, as this would be a two-hour stopover. Wendy and Jason walked down the gangplank, noticing many young men loading firewood onto their paddle wheeler to fuel the boiler. As they ventured away from the docks, people walked the dirt streets, everyone seeming to have a destination to go to.

Wendy and Jason walked by what resembled a restaurant. A sign in front of the ramshackle building advertised moose stew with fresh baked bread for sale. The couple went inside the building to eat, not wanting this rare opportunity to pass them by. The owner of the business was a friendly man, telling Jason and Wendy he had a friend who sometimes brought him fresh moose meat during the summer. He made stew with some and smoked a large portion of the meat in a smoker he had built out back. Tomorrow, he would offer the smoked moose for lunch instead of the stew.

The cook's creations from this kitchen never resulted in any food left over, as a steady stream of riverboats came and went from the docks, most stopping to pick up firewood. After eating this delicious meal, the couple still had some time to explore before needing to head back to the boat. While eating the stew, they had noticed a large cart of firewood being pulled to the dock by oxen. After a short walk they found the work yard, where logs were brought from the forest. The ox teams transported the wood here, where it was processed and then taken by an ox-pulled cart to the river.

The ship's whistle sounded, indicating the boat would be leaving shortly to continue its journey to Whitehorse.

The couple returned to the riverboat, which would not stop again until tomorrow, after lunch. Wendy and Jason prepared themselves for their long ride on the sometimes-unaccommodating Yukon River, a lifeline in Canada's north.

CHAPTER THIRTY-EIGHT

With a yell from Captain Barclay, the dock hands removed the lines which secured the riverboat to the dock. With two long toots from the ship's whistle, Barclay guided the riverboat away from the dock and back into the deeper water of the river. With the paddle wheel churning, the boat made its way through the turbulent waters of the Yukon River.

Wendy and Jason stood at the boat's railing, watching the activities on the dock they had just left, as it slowly disappeared from their vision. As the boat continued south, wilderness and the magic of nature surrounded the couple. A silence fell over the river, with only the occasional raptor's shrill cry heard, calling out for its soulmate.

Barges loaded with goods destined for Dawson were being pushed upriver by paddle wheel boats. This was the same way Samuel's goods would be transported from Whitehorse to Dawson. Suddenly, the quiet was interrupted by loud activity from the back of the boat. Yelling could be heard coming from a distressed passenger. Curious, Wendy and Jason walked towards where the commotion was originating from.

A young boy of around thirteen was struggling with two deck hands. He was a stowaway who was found hiding near the paddle wheel by the crew. The help was laughing at the boy's predicament, calling him "Junior", as they put a mop in his hand and instructed him to swab the decks until they reached Whitehorse. The captain arrived on scene, explaining this was the boy's punishment for failing to pay his fare on the riverboat. When they reached their destination, he would be evicted from the ship, not allowed to ride on a riverboat again. The boy told Barclay the rules were foolish and meant to be broken, and he would not hesitate to be the first one to do it. Barclay chuckled at the boy's brazen behaviour, turning away from him and returning to the wheelhouse.

Wendy and Jason realized they were again hungry and decided to check out the canteen on board. This small café offered a limited selection of food for paying passengers, and unlike the dining room, was open from sunrise to sunset. The couple entered, looking for something to quell the grumbling in their stomachs. They purchased two bowls of chicken soup, a delicious broth filled with fresh cut carrots and onions. The soup was served with fresh bread, just what the couple needed to fulfill the wishes of their hungry stomachs.

When Jason and Wendy were finished eating, they returned to their stateroom. The couple laid down on the bed, wrapping their arms around each other. The rocking of the riverboat as it slowly made its way down the river, made this moment even more romantic. Jason and Wendy were enjoying the peace and quiet, finding it unusual to have no chores or a child needing their attention. Suddenly, they were disturbed by loud shouting and a rush of activity outside their door. Concerned at this new development, Jason told Wendy to wait for him in the safety of their room as he went outside to investigate.

During recent flooding along the river, large trees had been displaced, their root systems washed bare by flood waters. These navigational hazards were washed into the river by the swift current. A lookout had been posted to keep watch for dangerous objects in the water, as colliding with large debris could cause serious damage to, or even sink, a paddle wheel boat. The spotter had observed a large, intact tree trunk lazily floating in the current towards the *Yukon Princess*. The crew had alerted the captain, who changed the boat's course to avoid a collision. Relieved at the positive outcome of what could have become a dangerous situation, Jason returned to his room to tell Wendy what the ruckus was about. He crawled back into bed, hoping to continue an uninterrupted nap with his wife. Quiet returned to the boat again, with only the sound of nature prevailing in this land called the Yukon.

CHAPTER THIRTY-NINE

Joe and Mary, along with their charge, Kuzih, were sitting on a blanket in the meadow by Wendy and Jason's home, enjoying a picnic lunch. They had taken the donkeys from the barn to graze on the lush green grass which grew in abundance there. A beautiful sunny day prevailed, causing Baby Jack, the youngest of the donkeys, to lay down and sleep in the warm sunshine. Kuzih expended some excess energy, running around the meadow with King, the family dog, in tow. Before returning the donkeys to the barn, Kuzih took a ride on the back of Baby Jack, who was no longer a baby. Baby Jack, like his father Omar before him, loved young children and was more than happy to entertain them when the opportunity arose.

Led by Mary, Baby Jack, with a laughing Kuzih riding on his back, headed back to his stall in the barn. After securing the happy animals, who all had full bellies, the trio exited the barn, telling Kuzih they were going to walk into Dawson. The couple needed to pick up a variety of household items from the general store. While there, they would let Kuzih pick a sweet from the candy counter. Afterwards, Joe wanted to stop by the livery stable, to pick

After the Gold Rush 109

up some mash for the donkeys. The animals considered this food a special treat.

Kuzih missed his mother and father, often asking Joe and Mary when they would be returning home. Joe and Mary tried to keep the child entertained so he would not miss Wendy and Jason as much. As the days passed, he would become less anxious about the fact his parents were not there.

Walking home, Joe noticed a bear cub imprisoned in a large structure made of wood. This homemade bear pen sat in the backyard of a house they passed on their way back home. Either the bear cub was an orphan because its mother had been shot for food, or the animal had been abandoned. If a mother bear gives birth to two cubs, she may be unable to properly care for them, without the tragic loss of both. In this circumstance, she would abandon the weaker of the two, ensuring the life of the healthy one.

Kuzih loved the bear cub, who looked lovingly at the child through the slats of his prison walls. He wanted to pet it, which Joe quickly vetoed. He explained to the child the cub was still a wild animal and could not be treated as a pet. Joe and Mary, carrying their purchases, soon found themselves at Jason and Wendy's, opening the front door. The air in the house smelled fresh and clean, as the crisp Yukon air flooded in through the open windows.

Mary started a fire in the woodstove to boil water. After putting away their purchases and sitting for a cup of coffee, Joe and Mary planned on taking Kuzih for a canoe ride on the lake. The child was an avid swimmer and loved going in the canoe. Jason had been teaching his son to use a paddle while in the craft, a skill he had not yet mastered.

The lake was calm, its crystal blue waters glistening in the sunshine. Kuzih did well sitting still in the front of the canoe. He pointed out the wildlife he saw, as the canoe slid across the calm waters of the open lake. Mary used her net and soon had enough fish in the bottom of the canoe to feed both man and dogs for dinner. They returned to the house, where Joe began to clean the fish Mary would cook on the woodstove. Joe would feed the sled dogs a healthy meal of whitefish for dinner, ensuring the survival of Jason's huskies, a commodity in the Yukon a man could not do without.

CHAPTER FORTY

The constant rocking of the boat in the water made it difficult to sleep in the stateroom. Wendy and Jason climbed out of the small bed. They left their room, walking out onto the open spaces of the riverboat, almost colliding with the stowaway who was mopping the deck. The main dining area on the boat served lunch and dinner, but only during selected hours. Tonight's special was fried chicken, roasted potatoes, a vegetable, and bread. Wendy and Jason decided to eat dinner, as they both liked fried chicken but rarely cooked it that way at home. The couple preferred their chicken baked in the oven or cooked slowly on a spit over an open campfire.

After eating dinner, the couple walked up the stairs to the top deck, where there was open seating for passengers. They found a bench to sit on, where they could see what was in front of them, as the vessel made its way down the river toward Whitehorse. Wendy and Jason claimed this seat as their own. The night was warm, with a light breeze caressing the faces of the couple. A full moon and shining stars lit a path for the riverboat to follow.

Wendy sent Jason back to their room to retrieve a

blanket. If the night stayed warm and dry, the couple would cuddle and sleep on the bench overnight. The rhythm of the paddlewheel churning the waters of the river behind them dominated all sound rising from the river. Other paddleboats, their whistles blaring, passed the *Yukon Princess* going the opposite direction, toward Dawson. Wendy and Jason slept peacefully on the bench that night, with Wendy's mother's blanket pulled snugly around them.

When they awoke the following morning, the couple's eyes were greeted by a beautiful red sky. Wilderness surrounded them, making Wendy and Jason feel alone in a strange land. They got up from the bench they slept on, stretching their cramped arms and legs, and made their way down to the canteen to find something for breakfast. Hot bread, fresh from the oven, and jam to spread on it was all the food they had to offer. A delight not passed up by Wendy and Jason, who both had a sweet tooth for jam. The baker working in the kitchen told the couple they would be stopping at a small settlement in four hours to take on wood. This would be their last stop, until they reached Whitehorse during the late afternoon.

CHAPTER FORTY-ONE

The rest of the couple's journey to Whitehorse was uneventful. The riverboat arrived at its destination with no mishaps or delays on its journey here from Dawson. Wendy and Jason gathered their belongings and exited the boat, wishing Captain Barclay a good day. Samuel had made reservations for them at a hotel in Whitehorse for the night. The couple had train tickets to Skagway for tomorrow, where they were headed to meet the ship travelling from Portland, Oregon with Samuel's order. Wendy and Jason were expected to take charge of these valuable goods and ensure their safe passage to Dawson. The manifest contained a variety of ironware, including updated cast iron woodstoves, large iron pots, frying pans, and anything made of iron used around the cabin, house, or barn. All items had been produced at a factory in Portland, the only foundry of its kind on the west coast at the time.

Wendy and Jason hired a driver with a horse and buggy to take them to their hotel from the dock. The couple found these new surroundings unlike those found in Dawson City. Whitehorse was a much more civil place than the frontier setting they were from. The driver dropped the couple off at their hotel, wishing them good luck on their endeavour and a safe journey home. Jason and Wendy entered the hotel and walked to the front desk. After registering, they were given a key and escorted to their accommodations upstairs, a well-appointed room with a balcony overlooking the street. The couple realized they were in downtown Whitehorse, by all the activity in the stores and shops below them on the street.

The couple had a bath, one of the luxuries offered at this upscale establishment. Afterwards they laid on the soft bed, not wanting to get up unless they had to. The happy couple fell asleep, not waking until after the sun had set. Wendy and Jason pulled themselves out of bed, dressed, and went downstairs to the dining room to eat dinner. The dining area was opulent, with beautiful table linens and waiters wearing white shirts and black bow ties. This was a world Wendy had not experienced before, and one Jason had not been in for years. They enjoyed a fabulous buffet of meat and vegetables, cooked fresh hours before in the hotel kitchen. There was also a large assortment of puddings, pies, and cakes on display for dessert.

After the couple ate their fill from the delicious buffet, they returned to their room upstairs. Tomorrow was an important day for the couple and being well-rested and prepared for it were more important than sight-seeing. Rest was on the couple's menu for tonight. The saloon on the street below was noisy until closing, when quiet settled over the town of Whitehorse. Jason and Wendy managed to sleep through the noise, wrapped together in each other's arms.

CHAPTER FORTY-TWO

A knock at the couple's hotel room door caused Jason and Wendy to stir. It was the wake up call they had requested from the front desk the night before. Wendy and Jason got up, dressed, and left the room, heading downstairs to enjoy a breakfast of bacon and eggs in the dining room. Before departing from the hotel, they placed their luggage in the baggage room to be stored overnight. The couple would return to the *Golden Horseshoe Hotel*, which had served them well, on their return from Skagway, Alaska.

Wendy and Jason took a horse and buggy from the hotel to the train station, carrying just a knapsack with a few essentials. They hoped their journey to Skagway would be a fast trip, with a turnaround of one day before their return trip to Whitehorse. Samuel's goods were to be transferred from the ship to a railcar, which would be picked up from the train yard when the couple was ready to depart Skagway for Whitehorse.

Jason and Wendy boarded the train. After a short wait, and with a long, loud whistle, the locomotive pulled away from the station, smoke billowing from its smokestacks. The train ride through the wilderness on this mechanical marvel was something the couple had not experienced before. The last time Jason had crossed this mountain pass, it was on foot. The tracks had just been completed this year, creating an experience which seemed more like a dream than reality.

After several short stops, the train pulled into Skagway, six hours after leaving Whitehorse, Jason and Wendy checked with the rail master, who assured them Samuel's order was secured on a rail car sitting in their yard. He said the car would be attached to the train and ready to leave Skagway for Whitehorse in the morning. The couple thanked the man, saying they would be on the train to Whitehorse, accompanying the goods. In Whitehorse, the ironware for Samuel's store would be transferred to a barge, which would be pushed up the Yukon River by a river boat to Dawson.

Wendy and Jason slept on a bench at the rail station, not wanting to miss the train to Whitehorse in the morning, and perhaps losing Samuel's order. The couple's sleep was restless and uncomfortable, but soon morning came. With a shrill blast of the whistle and plumes of rising smoke from the smokestacks, the train pulled out of the station for the six-hour journey to Whitehorse. Wendy and Jason laid back in their chairs, resting their weary souls in the comfort of the train seats.

Suddenly, the screaming of the train's brakes jolted the couple awake. The train continued braking, until it came to a complete stop on the tracks. Short blasts from the train whistle broke the silence which surrounded them. The conductor came through their car, explaining to the passengers a bull moose was on the tracks, refusing to move.

He told the smiling people they would have to wait until the moose was ready to move on his own, unless one of them would like to approach the moose and shoo him off the track. There were no volunteers for that suggestion.

After a brief time, the train started moving again, as the large animal lumbered back into the forest. The rest of the trip was uneventful, with the buildings of Whitehorse soon coming into view. The train tracks had been built to the port in Whitehorse, making the transfer of goods from rail to a barge relatively easy.

Disembarking from the train, Jason gave instructions about the transfer of goods to the barge. He told the men in charge at the dock, if all the goods arrived in Dawson undamaged, a substantial bonus would be paid to those responsible for accomplishing this important job. The dockmaster assured Jason the barge would be loaded and ready to leave for Dawson in the morning. With this task accomplished, the couple returned to the *Golden Horseshoe Hotel*, where they would spend the night.

CHAPTER FORTY-THREE

At daybreak, hotel staff knocked on Wendy and Jason's door, as the couple wanted to get up early, allowing them enough time to eat breakfast at the hotel before returning to the dock. A paddleboat, called the *Yukon Queen*, would be pushing the barge with the load of ironware products for Samuel's new store up the river to Dawson. After eating breakfast, the couple gathered their belongings and checked out of the hotel. They hired a horse and buggy, telling the driver to take them to the dock. A short ride later, they reached their destination, Jason paying the driver for the ride and wishing him a good day. The man drove the horse and buggy a short distance before stopping to pick up another fare to take back to the hotel the couple had just come from.

Wendy and Jason checked Samuel's load on the barge. The men had done a good job of securing the wares, covering them to keep them dry on the long four hundred mile trip up the river to Dawson City. Within an hour of the couple's arrival, the *Yukon Queen* was ready to leave the dock. The ten minute departure whistle sounded, prompting the last passengers to hurry aboard the vessel before it left without them.

From the deck, Jason and Wendy watched as the dockhands removed the ship's lines from the cleats attached to the dock. With a long toot of the boat's whistle and with the paddle wheel churning, the *Yukon Queen* left the dock on its journey to Dawson. Pushing a barge loaded with goods up the river was a formidable task, left for the most experienced captains. Such men had plied the river for years, earning an honest living and deep respect.

Jason and Wendy stayed on the deck, watching the forests pass by on either side of the riverboat. The wilderness stretched for hundreds of miles, with no large towns or settlements to be seen. The couple's journey was long and tiring, the barge slowing the riverboat down to a lower speed than normal, prolonging an already long journey. This paddle wheeler did not offer as many creature comforts as the *Yukon Princess*, making the trip seem even longer.

On the seventh day of the voyage, dusk was approaching when the outline of buildings could be seen in the distance. A sigh of relief swept over the couple when they realized their hard journey would soon be over. The men on the dock in Dawson grabbed the lines of the *Yukon Queen* and helped the captain dock the boat. The boat and barge were secured to the shore, allowing the passengers to disembark from the craft. The *Yukon Queen* would be docked in Dawson for two days, as they reloaded the barge with goods to take back to Skagway; snowshoes, sled parts, and dogsleds were some of the goods manufactured in town, as it diversified after the initial gold rush.

Wendy and Jason immediately headed for home, anxious to see their son, Kuzih, and Joe and Mary who had been taking care of him, their property, and their animals. Tomorrow morning, they would go to Samuel's store in Dawson, which Jason hoped was finished and ready to be furnished with the goods from the Portland foundry. They would return with Omar to pick up their personal belongings tomorrow, as well.

The couple were pleased they had completed their journey, a successful venture which would help Dawson grow by assisting in the establishment of a new business. This was not an easy job when living in the far north, which usually only extends hardships in a brutal and unforgiving land.

CHAPTER FORTY-FOUR

Jason and Wendy walked home from the Yukon River, where the paddleboat had docked, glad to be off the boat and walking on dry land. Entering their property, a jubilant King, the family dog, ran enthusiastically toward the couple, upon seeing them. With his tail wagging and the dog whining happily, King was glad to see his family was home.

Hearing the activity outside the house, Joe and Mary went to investigate. They were surprised to see Jason and Wendy, the couple playing with a happy dog who was glad to see his owners back from their absence. It was obvious King had missed Jason and Wendy very much while they were away. Seeing Jason and Wendy, Mary returned to the inside of the house and scooped up Kuzih, taking him outside to see who was here. The child's face shone with happiness at seeing his parents, as he reached out for them. Wendy and Jason wept; they were so happy to be holding their cherished son. The young child would not let go of his mother, who he continued to hug tightly.

The group walked into the house. Wendy and Jason were hungry, not having eaten nutritious or delicious food during the last six days. The food onboard the *Yukon Queen* was bland and unappetizing, usually meaning passengers were left hungry if they did not have the foresight to bring food on the boat with them. Wendy walked to the chicken coop, which was attached to the barn, and collected fresh eggs. Along with fried potatoes and hot baked bread and jam, it was the perfect meal for Jason and Wendy to enjoy after the long trip back from Skagway, Alaska.

In the morning, Joe and Jason led Omar, Jason's donkey, to the waterfront to retrieve Wendy and Jason's personal belongings from the boat. The women stayed behind with Kuzih, who still did not want to let his mother out of his sight. Before heading to the docks, the men went to find Samuel, wanting to inform him his order was safely sitting on a barge, in Dawson. Joe told Jason he had heard rumours the store was ready to be stocked, and customers were waiting for Samuel's goods to be delivered.

Upon seeing the store, Jason was amazed at the progress which had been made in the short time he was gone. A large sign hung proudly over the entranceway, advertising the new business as, "Samuel's Cast Iron Creations". In front of the store was a banner, which read, "Grand Opening Soon". When he saw Jason, Samuel knew his worries were over. Jason told the thankful man his merchandise had been safely delivered to Dawson and it was waiting at the docks. He asked Samuel to accompany him to the barge, where he could talk to the dockmaster about moving the product from the dock to his store.

After consulting with the dockmaster, Samuel was informed it was up to him to arrange delivery to the store,

After the Gold Rush 123

and he could not expect help from the dock workers. The dockmaster was all business, and not overly friendly, telling Samuel the barge needed to be unloaded within thirty-six hours, as it was scheduled to depart for Whitehorse at that time. He did refer Sam to a company for hire which could move his wares from the dock to the store using oxen and large wagons, giving him the business' card before saying goodbye and walking back to his office.

Samuel told Jason and Joe he needed to track down the man who owned the transport company immediately. He realized there was a very short time frame for getting his new merchandise off the barge and into his store. Jason said he understood, and they were picking up the luggage which had been left with the dockmaster last night. He told Samuel they would stop by the store after lunch, to see if they could be of any assistance with the move.

Samuel said goodbye to Jason and Joe, telling them he hoped to see them later. With that, Sam turned and left to look for the moving company the dockmaster told him about. Jason retrieved his belongings, tipping the dockmaster for taking care of the couple's personal items.

CHAPTER FORTY-FIVE

Joe and Jason led Omar, with his back loaded, toward home. It was a short walk and Jason was soon unloading Omar's back at the house. He then returned Omar to the barn, visiting with Honey and Baby Jack, the other two donkeys who lived there. All the donkeys were given a treat before Jason locked up the barn and left. Returning to the house, Jason gave the women an update on the store.

Both Wendy and Mary were anxious to shop for some new and updated ironware which Samuel now had available. Expecting a rush on his product, Samuel had already ordered more stock to be delivered before the river froze up. All boat traffic in and out of Dawson would cease in late fall, only resuming the following spring, when the ice melted, and the river would become navigable again. Samuel's brother would be accompanying the next order, as he was planning to stay in this frontier town and help his brother run the store.

After lunch and a brief nap, Jason and Joe returned to town. The men were surprised at what they saw as they approached the new ironware store. A crowd of curious bystanders were watching men unloading a large wagon being pulled by two oxen. A smiling Samuel was showing

After the Gold Rush 125

the workers where to place the larger items in the store. The more manageable items were placed aside, to be sorted and put on the shelves later. Within an hour, a second team joined the moving job and by late afternoon everything had been moved from the barge to the store. Two more days of unpacking, sorting, and placing the items on display for customers to see and feel, was all that were needed before the store's grand opening. The people in Dawson were eager to have access to this needed merchandise, waiting anxiously for Samuel's store to open.

Samuel promised Joe any merchandise they purchased now could be stored for them until Jason was able to deliver it with his dog team, the timing of which would depend on when the snows came, and the lakes froze enough for safe travel with the dogsleds. When Joe and Jason returned to the house, Joe and Mary decided they would wait two more days before returning home, as they wanted to be in town when the store opened.

Wendy suggested to Mary they should go fishing and try to catch enough food for dinner tonight for themselves and their dogs. Jason and Joe thought that was a great idea, saying they would stay and clean the donkeys' pens and dog yard while the women caught dinner. If successful, Jason would cook the fish and the group would eat the succulent fillets around the campfire tonight. Kuzih decided to let his mother go in the canoe with out him, as he wanted to stay with his father and work in the barn.

The wives' fishing trip was successful; they caught enough fish to feed all the hungry people and dogs, with some left over for tomorrow. Jason and Joe cleaned and filleted the lake trout, feeding the remains to King and Rusty, a meal these spoiled dogs never turned down. Wendy picked some fresh vegetables from the garden, green beans, and baby carrots, to eat with the fish. Mary worked on making strawberry cobbler for dessert.

Jason lit the campfire early, to allow it to burn down, producing the right heat to cook the fish. Wendy, Joe, and Mary, took Kuzih with them and walked to the lake to watch the sunset. This was one of child's favorite things to do, always asking someone to take him to the lake every night. Tonight, the view of the setting sun was spectacular, the sky turning multiple shades of red, orange, and pink.

The campfire's wood crackled, its flame casting light over the darkening landscape. The skywatchers returned from the lake, just as Jason yelled the fish was cooked. Wendy and Mary went into the house, grabbing the cooked vegetables from the woodstove to serve with dinner. Their meal was also accompanied by bread Wendy had baked earlier.

The evening was warm and breezy, the sky clear and full of stars. The Yukon night was captivating, sending the star gazers into a false sense of security. The serenity they felt at this time could never be taken from them, a secret they shared only with the Yukon.

CHAPTER FORTY-SIX

In the morning, the couples were surprised to find Samuel knocking on their door. Samuel, aware of Joe and Mary's wait for his store's grand opening, had come to Jason and Wendy's home to invite everyone in the house to shop early before he opened the doors to the public. In addition, because of Wendy and Jason's assistance ensuring his wares arrived safely, and Joe and Mary's help in watching Kuzih, he offered both couples a discount on anything they purchased.

Wendy made coffee for everyone, after which the two couples followed Samuel back to his store. Wendy and Mary purchased up-to-date cookware, including a cast iron kettle, pots, and a new frying pan for each of them. Mary also purchased new fireplace utensils, as Joe always told his wife the ones they had were original to when their cabin had been built. Joe bought a new axe and saw for cutting firewood. These new tools were stronger and less likely to break when used for heavy work than the older ones he had at the cabin. The handles of the tools were made of stronger wood, resulting in a tool that should last twice as long as what would be considered normal. Joe took his tools with him, but the kitchen utensils would need to be picked up later, as they were too heavy to be carried home.

After the couple's finished their shopping, they returned to Wendy and Jason's home. The group ate the left-over lake trout for lunch. Joe and Mary decided to leave for home today, as they could easily get there by late afternoon. Jason told them he would pick up their cookware and store it for them until they made it back to town. Mary and Joe gathered up their belongings and their dog Rusty. Saying goodbye to Wendy and Jason, they kissed Kuzih, telling the proud parents they had never seen a better-behaved child.

As the couple left Dawson for the three hour walk home, Wendy and Jason watched as they disappeared out of sight on the trail which led deep into the forest. For a moment, Wendy and Jason were thankful their fur trapping days were over since their move to Dawson. It was a life neither Jason nor Wendy missed.

CHAPTER FORTY-SEVEN

The piercing crow of the rooster woke Jason and Wendy at daybreak. The couple did not usually hear the rooster crow as loudly as he had this morning. Jason said it must be a cue for them to wake up early today. Wendy got out of bed, heading downstairs to fire up the woodstove, planning to boil water for coffee. King was glad to see someone stirring earlier than usual, not having to wait to be let outside.

Today, the couple planned to investigate a large shed on their property, which had been locked up since Bev's husband died. Bev's late husband had used the shed for cleaning fur when he was a trapper, but it later became a storage unit for his personal belongings. When Jason and Wendy first moved to Dawson, they never felt right about going through the belongings of Bev and her long-deceased husband. However, as time passed, the couple had become curious of what was in the shed Bev's late husband had used daily.

After breakfast, the couple joined King outside and walked over to the shed. A large padlock secured the front door, sending Jason to the woodshed to retrieve the axe.

He thought he could easily knock the padlock off the door by hitting it with the back of an axe. Jason approached the building, and with one hard whack from the axe, the lock fell to the ground. Splintered wood was all that remained where the lock once stood.

Jason pushed the door open, and the couple went inside. A musty smell greeted their senses, as well as the sight of cobwebs so thick the interior of the shed looked like it had been overrun by spiders, who had been dwelling in it undisturbed for years. Kuzih did not like the smell or look of the place, opting to stay outside with King to play.

Everything a fur trapper would need to run a successful trapline was stored in the shed. One piece which caught Wendy and Jason's attention was a dogsled Bev's husband had built from wood he had found on his property. Jason suggested they should donate the dogsled to the new museum in town. A man had opened it recently and had a display of artifacts from the area. This dogsled would make a perfect item to be included in his collection, as well as some early steel traps they pulled out of a pile which sat in the corner of the shed.

Searching further, the couple found a rifle, full of rust caused by sitting idle too long and two pairs of snowshoes built by members of Bev's tribe. A bowie knife, a saw for cutting bone, boards for stretching hides, and numerous other items needed for living life in the Yukon were scattered about the shed. After finding nothing more of interest, the couple headed outdoors. Jason nailed the door shut, so it would not blow open in the wind. They gathered Kuzih and made their way to the barn to feed the donkeys and chickens. When finished with these tasks, the family would return to the house, and with King, the family dog, spend the rest of the day relaxing in their home in the woods.

CHAPTER FORTY-EIGHT

The mid-August night was cool, which meant Jason would need to add wood to the woodstove and close the windows in the house before turning in. As the fall approached, the amount of daylight hours had grown shorter, with the nights getting colder. Wendy had added extra blankets to the beds the couple and their young son slept in upstairs. Her thoughts turned to the young men coming from her tribe to cut a supply of firewood for the couple. This fuel, for the stove and fireplace, would keep them and their son, Kuzih, warm during the cold months of winter.

King loved this time of year, as his spot by the woodstove was well heated by the warmth emanating from the fire, making him feel relaxed and comfortable. This was especially true after any encounter with the outdoors during the cooler months. King was not your average husky, preferring the summertime over winter. His love in life was sleeping by a warm fire, not being outside in the snow with his feet cold.

Wendy and Jason's dinner consisted of vegetables from Wendy's garden. The all-you-can-eat salad consisted of lettuce, carrots, onions, tomatoes, and radishes picked fresh from the garden. King ate dry dog food which had been purchased in Dawson at the livery stable. Jason's other huskies, who lived outside, were nourished with the same food tonight for dinner as King.

The evening was dark, with a cloud-filled sky. After dinner, the couple, their son, and King went for a walk to the lake. The couple sat in their favorite spot, with Kuzih sitting on his mother's lap while King snuggled affectionately into Jason's chest. The night was still, except for an occasional unidentifiable sound from the lake, which disrupted the silence which surrounded them. After spending an hour in quiet thought, the group left the serenity of the lake, returning to the comfort of their house. On the short walk there, an unexpected, stiff breeze blew through the tops of the tall trees which lined the path home. The sound of thunder broke through the silence of night, flashes of lightning illuminating the waters on the lake.

The glow of the oil lamps caused the home to emit an eerie light into the darkness. Wendy, Jason, Kuzih, and King entered the building. Within minutes, torrential rainfall could be heard outside, giving life a drink of nourishing water. Inside, it was dry and comfortable, the wood crackling in the fireplace creating a feeling of comfort and belonging in their wilderness home. The storm passed leaving the quiet of the forest to take over. Only the sound of Mother Nature's raindrops could be heard dripping from the trees high above. A constant trickle from the eaves of the roof was like a never-ending song, a song meant to calm the spirits of souls who chose to live in this chaotic land called the Yukon.

CHAPTER FORTY-NINE

During the night, many animals visited Wendy and Jason's property. Hungry wildlife looking for food, was the most common reason these forest inhabitants were drawn here. Occasionally, a bear would show up, having caught the scent of the donkeys which resided in the barn. Unable to gain entry and enjoy this delectable meal, the large predator would leave in frustration, much to the relief of Omar and his family who were locked securely inside.

Unbeknown to Wendy and Jason, a pair of foxes had dug a den under a fallen tree trunk a short distance from their house. The foxes were the most common visitors to come at night, always looking for dropped food around the smoker or campfire. Always curious was the skunk, who often waddled around the grounds near the house, looking for any food he might come upon. If unsuccessful, the skunk would dig for grubs in Wendy's garden, searching for his favorite snack.

The morning sun shone through the bedroom window, waking Wendy and Jason from their undisturbed slumber. King barked from downstairs, wanting to be let outside. Jason pulled himself out of bed to go grant King's wish.

After breakfast, Wendy and Jason planned to walk into Dawson City to visit Samuel at his Cast Iron Creations store. Kuzih always looked forward to visiting town, as he perpetually seemed to see something of interest while there.

The day was sunny and warm, with a light breeze which caressed the faces of the couple as they walled to Samuel's store. Dogs in the backyards of the homes they passed, barked loudly and aggressively when Jason and Wendy walked by. Reaching Sam's shop, it seemed unusually quiet, with few people around. Walking inside, they realized why. Samuel had sold out of most of his stock during his grand opening sale. The demand for his wares had grown, as the city of Dawson grew.

Samuel, always happy to see them, told Jason his brother should be arriving with another barge load of ironware products within the next week. This would be the last shipment to arrive from the foundry before winter. Deliveries would resume when the riverboats could once again travel the open waters of the Yukon River in the spring. Sam told Jason unless he could think of another use for his ironware store, he would be closing it for the winter due to a lack of product to sell. He expected the next order he received would be sold out before the first snows came to Dawson. He was giving serious consideration to leaving town, going south to Seattle with his brother and returning to Dawson in the spring. After a brief conversation, Samuel told Jason and Wendy if he made the decision to leave for the winter he would stop at their house and tell them.

The group said their goodbyes, with Wendy and Jason walking to the livery stable to pick up food for their sled dogs and donkeys. Walking home, Wendy and Jason were stopped on the street by an old prospector and his donkey. Downtrodden and starving, Jason felt sorry for this man, inviting him back to their home for a meal and a bath. The man's name was Johnson, and he was most grateful for Wendy and Jason's hospitality. He told them he was penniless and starving, and kindly accepted their offer.

CHAPTER FIFTY

Johnson and his donkey, Millie, followed Wendy and Jason to their home. Upon arriving, Jason and Johnson took Millie to the barn to feed her and get her settled into a pen with clean straw. Millie was not in good health, as she had been trying to survive in the bush with the old prospector. She had survived three attacks by predators and had been saved each time through the quick actions of Johnson and his rifle.

Omar and his family were thrilled about Millie joining them in the barn. Donkeys are social animals, who enjoy living in large groups, making it easy for them to cohabitate with one another successfully. The men returned to the house to enjoy the hot coffee Wendy had made while they were in the barn. Johnson said he had come to Dawson from Vancouver after divorcing his wife and did not know, or have, any friends or family in the area. He had purchased a donkey and headed into the wilderness to seek his fame and fortune. After enduring many hardships, and the three attacks by hungry predators on Millie, Johnson gave up on his adventure, making his way back to Dawson with no gold and no money.

Wendy showed Johnson to a bedroom upstairs and supplied him with a pitcher of hot water for him to wash up with. After completing this task, Johnson returned downstairs to the aroma of something delicious cooking. Wendy was frying a piece of venison which Samuel had given her earlier this morning. He had shot a young doe yesterday and was giving the extra meat to whomever would eat it before it spoiled from lack of refrigeration. Johnson was thankful to be sitting at a table in a comfortable house, after spending weeks in the bush alone.

After eating his first meal in days, the old prospector told Wendy and Jason of his plans. He wanted to return to Vancouver, where he had family whom he hoped would help him. Johnson asked Wendy and Jason if they were interested in purchasing Millie, his donkey. Feeling sorry for the man, Wendy and Jason agreed to buy Millie, knowing he could not take her with him to Vancouver. Recently enriched by their trip to Skagway, the couple offered the wayward traveller two days of work around their property. In exchange, Jason would assume responsibility for Millie, pay for Johnson's fare to Vancouver, and provide enough extra money to cover expenses, such as food, for his trip. Johnson readily agreed to these terms, thankful he had run into such a generous couple.

Over the next two days, Johnson worked hard on neglected jobs needing to be addressed on Jason and Wendy's property. Millie loved her home in the barn and the new friends she had made. The donkey's health began to improve quickly, with the fine care she was given by Jason and Wendy. Having finished his work at the couple's house,

After the Gold Rush 139

Johnson was anxious to be heading back to Vancouver. Jason had purchased passage on a boat heading to Whitehorse, which would take him partway home. From there, Johnson would take the train to the coast, where he would be able to find a ship headed to Vancouver.

Before heading to the docks in Dawson, Johnson went to the barn to say goodbye to Millie, knowing he would never see her again. He thanked Wendy and Jason for their help, walking away with his head up, instead of down. Johnson pictured a new life in front of him, after being treated so kindly by these two strangers he met on a dusty road in Dawson. This was the spirit of the Yukon, giving lost souls another chance at life.

CHAPTER FIFTY-ONE

The month of August was slipping away, which would soon mean big changes for the landscape. In the Yukon, because of its far north location, fall starts in early September. The beautiful colors of the summer wildflowers, which once filled the meadows, will be gone, the plants having lived through their life cycle during the growing season. The soul of the plant will retreat into the earth, until the warm sunshine the following spring restores life to the dormant vegetation hibernating in the frozen dirt.

Jason and Wendy were sitting in the kitchen drinking coffee when they heard a knock at the front door. Jason answered, asking the visitor to identify themselves. It was the two young men from Wendy's tribe, who the couple had hired to cut a supply of firewood to get them through the winter. The young men arrived with a mule, whose back held supplies for a week's stay. Wendy invited them in and brewed fresh coffee for them.

These same two brothers had worked for Jason and Wendy last year, completing the same task. One brother was named Little Beaver, while the older one was named Big Beaver. They were given these names because of their sizes at birth, which did not reflect the fact the younger brother now towered over his older sibling. Unfortunately for the brothers, other kids in the tribe made fun of the boys because of their unusual names when they were growing up. This whole debacle was created by their father, who had a reputation as an unusual man who lived with the tribe.

The two brothers would set up their camp in the meadow which was close to Jason and Wendy's house. Jason told the men there were now three adult pack animals in the barn they could use for moving wood. He asked them to not overload the animals, and not to use the youngest donkey, Baby Jack. Since the young men had been here last year, they were familiar with the property. Jason had to explain nothing more to them related to their work; the boys knew what to do.

The brothers finished their coffee and left the house to set up their camp. Little and Big Beaver worked hard over the next week cutting a winter's supply of firewood. Big Beaver made an unusual find one day, when cutting up a log with his brother. An old rusty pistol, which apparently someone had jammed into a hole in a tree trunk, was discovered after the brothers had harvested the wood. Jason told Big Beaver he could keep his find, as he had no idea who the rightful owner might be and considering the condition of the gun he doubted it had any real value.

A shower of leaves had begun falling from the deciduous trees, creating a blanket of multi-covered vegetation on the ground. The waterfowl on the lake were preparing for their long journey south, flocking together in groups, soon to leave in mass numbers for warmer waters. The young men finished the job for Wendy and Jason, telling the couple they hoped to see them next year for the same reason.

Inspecting their woodpile, along with the wood left over from last year, Wendy and Jason now had enough firewood piled up on their porch and in the woodshed to keep them warm all winter. Jason paid the young men for a job well done. The boys planned to go into Dawson to look at what was available for sale in Samuel's ironware store, as the barge containing more stock had arrived last week. The brothers would use the money they had earned to buy something useful for the tribe. The men broke down their camp loading their mule for the trip home. Jason and Wendy wished them well, watching as they walked to town, until the boys disappeared.

CHAPTER FIFTY-TWO

A fine mist hung over the calm waters of the lake as the morning sunrise painted the sky red. The soulful call of the loon completed this perfect wilderness picture set in the Yukon at the turn of the century.

Jason stirred in his bed, listening to the entertaining birdsong which was drifting through the open bedroom window. He woke his wife to hear the medley of music the birds were singing together. The sound captivated the couple, as they lay quietly in their bed listening. Then the music stopped, leaving the couple missing the joy created by the birdsong which had been silenced.

Wendy pulled herself out of bed, going downstairs to let King outside. She lit a fire in the woodstove, to boil water for coffee. Jason was soon awake and followed Wendy downstairs to the kitchen. Wendy had the coffee brewing, now that the water was hot. She joined Jason at the kitchen table to discuss their plans for the day. The couple decided to take King and Kuzih and work on the trail they had been clearing around their lake. The September day was sunny and warm, a perfect day for completing outside activities.

Kuzih, like his father, Jason, loved to be outside

breathing in the fresh air nature provided. Jason retrieved Millie from the barn and began to load some supplies on her back to take with them for the day. This would provide a good opportunity for Millie and her new owners to get to know each other better. With no complaint from Millie, Jason finished placing tools on her back and led the donkey from the barn, toward the trail which wrapped around the lake.

Wendy, Kuzih, and King joined Jason here at the start of the trail they had been clearing. The entourage walked to their destination, a half mile down the path. The job was laborious, but over a four-hour span they managed to clear another half mile of trail. Jason figured they were half done with the work he wanted to accomplish, but as it was past noon, he and Wendy were ready to call it a day.

Sudden barking from King caught their attention, causing Jason to walk into the woods off the trail to see what his dog had found. Jason was startled at what he saw, bones scattered everywhere. He called Wendy to come see what King had alerted them to. After examining the bones, Jason thought he had an explanation as to what created this backdrop of violence and death. A rusty rifle lay at the scene, along with pieces of tattered clothing. Apparently, a man had encountered a bear quite some time ago, with neither coming out the winner. Their bones lay scattered about, as a testament to their fight with each other.

Kuzih found the bleached skull of the bear and wanted the teeth, which were still attached to the animal's jaw. Jason removed the teeth and would carry them home for his son. Kuzih wanted to display the teeth with other unusual finds he had brought home from the forest. Wendy and Jason left this unusual scene as it was, not wanting to disturb the remains of the dead that lay scattered about. The Yukon had claimed two lives, having no regard for human or animal alike. Death can be quick and unexpected in this land, with the remains of the dead rarely found, a land where nature makes the rules.

CHAPTER FIFTY-THREE

After building the house, which Wendy and Jason now live in, Bev and her husband planted ten apple trees on their property. Over the years, the trees matured and produced a harvest of good fruit yearly. Wendy informed Jason they needed to harvest the apples, as they were ripe and if not picked would fall to the ground and rot. This would attract unwanted bears to the property, the aroma drawing them in to eat the delicious, rotting fruit.

Apples were the pioneers' best friend. If stored properly, they remain edible for months after being picked from the trees. Besides being nutritious when eaten raw as a snack, apples can be used in a variety of ways for cooking and baking desserts. The most famous dessert made by these early settlers was apple pie. Apple crisp, along with apple sauce, baked apples, stewed apples, apple cake, apple muffins, and the juice squeezed from the whole fruit were all popular uses for this versatile crop.

Wendy and Jason had made plans with Grey Wolf and Rose for them to come to Dawson and help harvest the fruit from their apple trees. When the harvest was finished, Jason would take Omar and Honey from the barn and use the donkeys to move some of the harvest to Grey Wolf and Rose's cabin in the bush. From there, the fruit would be distributed to other trappers and their families living throughout the forest. Wendy and Jason would travel to Grey Wolf and Rose's home and back to Dawson in a single day, to allow the donkeys to be safe in their barn by nightfall.

Coincidently, on this very day that Wendy and Jason were talking about harvesting the apples, Grey Wolf, Rose, and their dog, Charlie, arrived at their home. Wendy told the couple their timing could not have been better, as the apples were ready to be harvested and they could pick the fruit tomorrow. Rose thought it was lucky they had arrived when they did and the two of them were happy to begin the harvest.

Grey Wolf had shot two rabbits and a couple of grouse on his walk here. After visiting for a spell over coffee, the men went to the shed to clean Grey Wolf's prey for tonight's dinner. Kuzih wanted to stay with Jason and Grey Wolf, as he loved watching his father clean and prepare wild game to eat. While the men were busy, Wendy and Rose walked to the orchard to gather enough fruit to make an apple pie for dessert. King and Charlie, the two spoiled family dogs, entertained each other by chasing one another around the outside of the house.

After getting bored with their game, the two dogs wandered off into the forest, looking for a new adventure. While working in the shed cleaning the rabbits and grouse, Jason and Grey Wolf talked about the annual family moose hunt, which was coming up in November. The hunters would gather at Johnathan and Shining Star's cabin, a location with large areas of perfect habitat for moose. Johnathan's cabin was also spacious, with outbuildings for people to comfortably sleep in, if needed. The facilities on their property were well-suited for the processing of large game, such as moose and deer. This was a family event everyone looked forward to.

CHAPTER FIFTY-FOUR

Smelling the odor of fresh meat coming from the shed, King and Charlie returned from the woods, sitting outside begging for food. Kuzih teased the dogs with the inedible inners of the butchered animals, finally relenting and giving the hungry huskies what they perceived as a delectable delight. Wendy soon appeared, carrying a large pot of boiling water from the woodstove, she brought it for Jason to soak the grouse in, as this allowed for easier removal of the birds' feathers.

Finally finished cleaning and butchering the small game, Jason and Grey Wolf returned to the house. Opening the front door, they were greeted by the sweet smell of an apple pie with cinnamon baking. Jason had childhood memories of hot apple pies left on an open kitchen windowsill to cool. The sweet smell of cooked apples and pastry still draw him close, hoping to be offered a piece of this seasonal dessert. Wendy informed him he would have to wait until dinner, just like everyone else.

Apple harvest was a special time of year, as the fruit was an important food crop used in a variety of productive ways, including nutritious treats for the pack animals. Being denied dessert, Jason was ready to concentrate on dinner. The rabbit would be fried on the woodstove, with some onions and potatoes from Wendy's garden, while the grouse would be cooked over the campfire, where the group would eat dinner tonight. The men went outside to light the fire they would use to roast the grouse.

The foxes, who lived on the edge of the woods facing the house, had Jason under surveillance. These cunning mammals had been alerted to the possibility of fresh food, sensing the activity by the campfire. The dry wood made starting the campfire easy and soon a hot flame was reaching for the sky, smoke rolling into the forest. Jason let the wood burn down, as he wanted to cook the grouse over the hot embers. Grey Wolf prepared the birds for cooking, placing them over the now ready coals.

The aroma of the frying rabbit wafted through the open windows of the house, catching the hungry foxes' attention. As evening fell, the night was cold but pleasant. A full moon and a sky full of stars looked down upon the men as they finished roasting the meat. The group of friends and family sat together, enjoying the warmth from the campfire while listening to the sizzle of the grouse cooking over the open flame.

Enjoying their dinner and dessert under the night sky, the diners were thankful for this time together. The night grew long, causing Wendy to take Kuzih into the house shortly after eating. The rest of the group decided to call it a night shortly thereafter, retiring into the house. Before going inside, Jason, aware of his pets who lived under a tree trunk on the edge of the clearing, took two small pieces of leftover rabbit and laid them by the campfire for the grateful foxes to eat.

The sun shone brightly in through the windows, indicating a clear day had dawned. The air was crisp, like the apples the couples were picking today. After waking up, dressing, and eating a quick breakfast, the group headed out to the orchard with apples on the menu today. They began by picking the lower branches, placing all the fruit in canvas bags. They made sure to leave plenty of apples within Kuzih's reach, to keep him busy throughout the day.

Once they had gathered everything easily accessible, Jason and Grey Wolf climbed the trees and tossed down fruit, as they did not want it damaged. After this job was done, the trees were shaken, allowing the remaining fruit to hit the ground. These bruised apples would be turned into fine tasting apple cider. The group harvested more than enough apples for themselves and their extended families. The rest of the fruit was left for members of Wendy's tribe to harvest, always happy to receive as many apples as possible before winter.

Wendy, Jason, Grey Wolf, and Rose gathered the bags of apples, carrying them to the house where they would be stored in the basement. They placed fifty pounds of the fruit in two canvas bags, connected by a strap which slid over a pack animal's back, like saddle bags. Jason had decided to only take Omar on the journey to Grey Wolf's house, figuring he could carry twenty-five pounds of apples in each sack which would grace the sides of his protruding belly. These apples were locked in the shed in anticipation of their trip into the bush tomorrow.

Before retiring to the house, the group walked to the barn with a handful of apples to feed the donkeys. The animals loved the apples, which they enjoyed for a short time each year. They were a special gift for the always hungry donkeys, who constantly were looking for treats.

CHAPTER FIFTY-FIVE

The rest of the afternoon, the couples socialized together in the living room of the house. Jason lit a fire in the fireplace for ambience and comfort. The day had turned blustery and cold, with the arrival of a cold front from the north. King and Charlie jockeyed for position beside the fireplace, waiting for the flame to start the wood burning.

A sudden knock on the door abruptly changed the quiet afternoon the couples were enjoying together. Jason got up from his chair to answer his front door, happy to see Samuel, the owner of the ironware store in Dawson, standing on the other side. Jason invited him inside for coffee, the two men joining Wendy, Grey Wolf, and Rose in the living room. Samuel told Jason and Wendy he had decided to go to Seattle with his brother, Dave, to spend the winter. The latest load of stock for the store had already sold out, except for a few of the more unpopular items.

Samuel planned to keep his store open one more week and had already booked riverboat passage for himself and his brother to Whitehorse for the following week. He asked the couple if he could leave them a key to the store, wanting them to be able to get inside should an emergency arise.

Sam told the couple, he would stop at the North West Mounted Police detachment headquarters in Dawson to let the officers know of his plans, and who they should get in touch with if there was an emergency.

Aa Samuel had become a trusted friend, Jason and Wendy readily agreed to do this for him. Pleased, he told Jason and Wendy he would stop in to see them before leaving Dawson for Seattle. With his business here finished, Samuel left, shaking everyone's hand and wishing them luck in their future endeavours, before walking out the front door.

Jason told Wendy and their company he was going to walk into Dawson to purchase fish from the fish peddlers. This Indigenous man and his wife went fishing at dawn every morning, coming home only after their canoe was full of lake trout and whitefish. It was rare for this couple to have no fish for sale. Grey Wolf went with Jason, partly to go for the walk and to help carry the fish back from town. The afternoon was waning, with dusk beginning to settle over this frontier town.

Jason purchased the remaining fish the couple had not sold, which was mostly whitefish, with a few large lake trout. It was more than enough fish for dinner for everyone, including one whitefish for each sled dog. The couple's personal pets, King, and Charlie, would enjoy the remains of the lake trout after they were cleaned. This was the pampered huskies favorite parts of the trout to eat.

After Grey Wolf and Jason cleaned the fish, Wendy cooked the fillets inside on the woodstove. The cold blustery wind made it difficult for Jason to keep a campfire at a constant temperature to allow for cooking outside. Dinner was enjoyed by all, especially by King and Charlie, who gathered around the table for a second helping of fish. A dog's stomach is never satisfied, a bottomless pit that is impossible to fill.

CHAPTER FIFTY-SIX

The morning sun peeped above the horizon, with the promise of a sunny day. Grey Wolf and Rose were taking Charlie and walking back to their cabin in the forest today. They would be joined by Wendy, Jason, Kuzih, their dog, King, and Omar, the donkey who would be carrying fifty pounds of apples into the bush. Jason went to the barn to retrieve Omar, leading the donkey to the shed where Grey Wolf helped Jason load the apples on the donkey's back. To get Omar to cooperate, Jason fed him two of the apples out of the sack the pack animal would be carrying.

Jason led Omar and the entourage to the trail which led into the forest. The morning air was crisp, the night temperature having fallen to close to freezing. It was the beginning of October and soon the snow would come to the Yukon. At first, small amounts of snow would fall, followed by larger amounts as the fall progressed into winter. The group of travellers trudged on, with little conversation breaking the quiet of the forest which surrounded them.

Suddenly, a growl from King broke the silence. Jason stopped walking, taking the time to look around. A dark shape moving through the trees caught Grey Wolf's attention. He quietly told Jason a bear was following their party. Hibernating soon, the animal was looking to build up its fat reserves before going to sleep for the winter. This predator loved to eat pack animals, a favorite food if one could be found vulnerable in the forest. Grey Wolf and Jason agreed there was little chance the bear would attack before they reached Grey Wolf and Rose's cabin.

The rest of the journey through the forest was uneventful, the group reaching their destination without any encounter with the bear, who had followed closely behind them until the buildings of Rose and Grey Wolf's homestead were in sight. Jason led Omar to the shed, where the men unloaded the apples from his back. They then walked to the cabin, where the men joined their wives for a cup of coffee. Jason left Omar tied to the front porch and kept the cabin door open to ensure he was safe. Jason and Wendy could not visit long if they wanted to get home before dark.

Kuzih could have cared less about leaving for home, after discovering a whole new world to explore at Grey Wolf and Rose's cabin. After finishing their coffee, Wendy and Jason grabbed their unwilling son and their dog, King, to start their walk home. Thirty minutes into their walk on the trail, the dog once again alerted Jason to the bear, which was following them again. Jason felt this bear was hungry and could not be trusted to not attack Omar, if given the right opportunity. Jason's rifle was primed and loaded in case he needed to use it quickly.

Luckily, the bear had second thoughts about trying to attack Omar for food, giving up his pursuit, knowing it was too risky. Wendy, Jason, Kuzih, and King made it back to their home without incident, Kuzih allowed to ride Omar for the last half-hour of the trip. Jason put Omar back in the barn, much to the relief of his wife and child. They had been worried about him, fearing he may not return home safely from his dangerous trek through the wilderness of Canada's north.

CHAPTER FIFTY-SEVEN

Jason returned to the house, with King in tow. The sky was darkening as dusk spread across the land. A squirrel chattered loudly at King as he passed under the branches the animal was sitting on. King barked at the squirrel ferociously, displaying his annoyance with this animal. Wendy had started a fire in the woodstove, the crackling of the burning wood meant the house would be warm and cozy in a short time. Puffs of smoke rose from the chimney, as the fire took hold in the belly of the stove. King was glad to be home, as he had missed his favorite spot by the stove, where he was now lying.

The evening passed quietly by. After eating a bowl of vegetable soup with fresh baked bread, the couple retired to the living room. Bev's husband had kept a small library in the house, as collecting books and reading had become a passion for this man. He had accumulated over fifty books, which he had kept on shelving he had built along one wall of the living room. Wendy and Jason each chose a book from the collection to read. Jason chose a wilderness adventure story, while Wendy chose a book about an immigrant family struggling to survive in this new and rugged land called

Canada. The evening was dark and quiet, with only a light breeze rustling the leaves as it blew through the treetops surrounding the house.

After reading for an hour, the couple's eyes grew heavy and it became difficult to stay awake. They both set their books down and retired to the bedroom, where a peaceful night's sleep was in order. The lonely call of the night owl was the last thing the couple remembered hearing before drifting off. As the first hint of daylight filtered in through the bedroom window, Jason and Wendy stirred in their bed. King was downstairs barking, wanting to be let outside.

Jason reluctantly pulled himself out of bed, walking downstairs to let King out. Upon opening his front door, he was shocked at what he saw, a half-eaten deer lay at the far end of his front yard. Jason returned to the bedroom to get dressed, telling Wendy about the deer which had been killed by a predator, its half-eaten carcass lying in the front yard.

By the time Jason got outside, King was helping himself to the deer meat, on the ground for his taking. Jason shooed King away from the corpse, his muzzle covered with fresh blood as he moved away from the deer. Jason picked up the remains of the animal and carried it to the shed. He knew he could process a lot of the meat, which had not been eaten by the bear who had attacked and killed the deer.

Locking it in the shed, he returned to the house, joining his wife in the bedroom. Telling her they would be eating venison for dinner, Jason crawled back into bed, wrapping his arms tightly around his wife and going back to sleep. It was just another day in the Yukon, where one never knows what adventure will be waiting.

CHAPTER FIFTY-EIGHT

October is a month of transition in the north. The cold, grey sky will bring the first snowfall to the area. As the month progresses, so does the amount of snow received. By early November, the dogsleds will be pulled out of storage and readied for the winter season. The lakes will freeze into superhighways, the sled dogs can race on. Another trapping season will begin, in this land called the Yukon.

Jason got out of bed with the half-eaten deer on his mind. He woke Wendy and asked her if she could get the outdoor freezer ready to store meat in. He was anxious to take advantage of the gift nature had provided overnight. It was cool enough during the day to safely store meat, it was rare for the daytime highs to get above freezing. If the weather stayed cool, the meat could be preserved until it was ready to be cooked by the couple.

Jason went to work with his faithful dog, King, at his side. The bear had eaten half the deer, leaving the rest of his meal for another day. In four hours, the butchering was completed. Jason had salvaged what he estimated to be sixty pounds of meat from the mangled deer. King and the sled dogs would share the remainder of the carcass, which Jason had been unable to salvage for his family to eat.

While he had been working alone, Jason had come up with a plan. He knew the bear would most likely return, looking for the rest of the deer he had not eaten last night. Jason would lie in wait for the bear, shoot the animal, and store its meat in his outdoor freezer. Jason thought if he managed to secure more meat than they needed, they would give the excess away to native people who were hungry.

When Jason returned to the house, he told Wendy of his plan. He thought a tree stand in a large tree overlooking the front yard would provide a place for him to sit where the bear could not see him. Wendy thought it was good idea and should provide a great start to filling their outdoor freezer for the winter. She fried some of the fresh venison for lunch, the aroma of the meat cooking made Jason realize how hungry he was.

After lunch, Jason built the tree stand he would sit in to shoot the bear. He started the smoker and stocked it with some of the deer meat. He hoped the odor from the smoker would help draw in the bear to investigate the smell. He reached into the cupboard for heavy caliber shells for his rifle, as a full-grown male bear is not easy to kill without the proper ammunition.

Once everything was prepared, Jason laid down for a nap, not knowing how long he would be waiting for his prey to show up. Wendy would wake him after the day turned to night. With luck, the unsuspecting bear would be on the dinner menu tomorrow.

CHAPTER FIFTY-NINE

Wendy woke Jason from his nap. She had fried venison for dinner, served with potatoes and some of the last of the carrots from her garden. Jason's excitement mounted, as he thought about the bear hunt he was going to embark on later this evening. Waiting until darkness prevailed, he grabbed his rifle and kissed his wife goodbye. Wendy wished Jason luck and followed him to the front door. She told him to be careful and not make any stupid decisions which could cost him his life.

Jason walked from the house across the yard and climbed into his tree stand. He made himself comfortable, as he observed the property around him. Hours passed with no sign of the bear. Eventually, a slight rustling along the tree line caught Jason's attention. He watched as a large skunk came out of the woods and walked to the smoker. After a short investigation of the area, the skunk found nothing of interest, turning and retreating back into the forest.

Two more hours went by, Jason having fallen asleep sitting in the tree stand. Suddenly, he was abruptly awakened by a loud noise. Looking up he saw a large black bear come out of the forest walking toward him. He picked up his rifle, which had been lying across his stomach and released the safety. The bear walked into an open area in the yard, giving Jason a clear shot. Jason raised his gun, getting the unsuspecting bear in his sight. He aimed for the animal's heart as he fired off two shots in quick succession. The bear staggered forward. Jason shot a third time. The animal fell on the ground, lying motionless.

Jason exited the tree stand and walked toward the bear, even from a distance, seeing the animal was dead. Looking at the body, he figured the bear was a two-year-old male. He grabbed the animal by the hind legs and dragged it to the shed. He then secured the door and went back to the house, to a waiting Wendy. He related what had happened out in the yard, telling Wendy he had locked the body in the shed, where he would butcher the animal tomorrow and store the meat in the outside freezer. Jason washed up and the couple returned to bed.

When Jason got out of bed early in the morning to let King outside, he was met by a surprise, blowing snow in his face. Six inches of snow covered the ground. The weather had been growing progressively colder in the last two weeks, making Jason believe it was time for a snowstorm, but when he came to bed last night, there was little hint it would come upon them so quickly.

The calendar had changed to November, and in two weeks, the lakes would be frozen enough to allow the dogsleds to travel on them. The winter season was here, and this snow was just the bottom layer of much more to come. Jason returned upstairs to the bedroom, telling Wendy about the snowstorm which was raging outside. Wendy, not responding to Jason, rolled over and went back to sleep.

CHAPTER SIXTY

Black Hawk and White Dove had adjusted well to life in their new cabin. The lake and forest which surrounded them provided an ample supply of food. With their outside freezer cleaned out and ready to be filled with meat for the winter, and enough wood cut to last until summer, the couple felt they were well prepared for the harshest season of the year.

As promised, Black Hawk's father had brought the dogsled and team he had said he would give to his son and daughter-in-law. The dogs were fine huskies, all happily adjusted to living in the yard Johnathan had built for his own dog team. These fine animals would allow Black Hawk and White Dove to easily travel when snow was abundant, including going to Johnathan and Shining Star's cabin for the moose hunt with their dog, Nicky.

The moose hunt would be taking place soon, the hunters all preparing for this important early winter event. This was one of the few times each year all the friends and family got together. Jason and King were attending the hunt, while Wendy would stay home to take care of their son, Kuzih, and the donkeys which lived in the barn. Steward would be attending, but Blossom would also need to stay home to look after the huskies her husband bred and sold. Grey Wolf and Rose, along with Joe and Mary, would also be in attendance. Johnathan and Shining Star were going to have a full house, everyone living in a chaotic atmosphere for three or four days, depending on the success of the hunt.

Jason was packed, ready to go to Jonathan and Shining Star's cabin. He had promised the couple he would come a day early to help with any prep work for the hunt which needed to be done. He kissed Wendy and Kuzih goodbye, taking half of the bear meat with him. This would help feed the hungry crowd at Johnathan's house until the men shot a moose or deer to eat.

King ran alongside Jason's sled, keeping pace with the sled dogs, who Jason kept at a speed which would not tire King out quickly. After a long, uneventful trip, Jason's presence was announced by Johnathan's barking huskies. The couple came out of their cabin and greeted Jason, happy to see him again. Johnathan helped Jason unload his sled and was surprised to see the bear meat. Johnathan and Shining Star were short of food, making the meat a godsend for them.

Johnathan started the smoker, wanting to have food ready for when the rest of the hunting party and some of their wives showed up tomorrow. In the morning, Jason would help Johnathan do a few things to get ready for the hunt. But for the time being, the evening passed quickly. Dinner was a heaping serving of bear steak, fried to perfection on the woodstove.

Over dinner, Jason and Johnathan discussed the moose hunt, with Johnathan telling Jason he had his sights on a bull moose a few days ago in an area which was thirty minutes by dogsled from the house. Johnathan believed the moose had settled into the area for the winter, as it provides plenty of food and shelter for the animal's survival. The men retired to bed early, wanting to be well rested before a busy day tomorrow. They were both anxious for the arrival of their family and friends, for what they hoped would be a big adventure.

CHAPTER SIXTY-ONE

Johnathan and Shining Star's expected company arrived at various times over the course of the day. Steward was the last one to arrive, having left late because of an incident with one of his sled dogs. He arrived just as the sun was setting below the horizon. It was mayhem at Johnathan's house, with sled dogs barking, men unpacking supplies from their sleds, family dogs running around, and everyone talking.

Black Hawk had been put in charge of the smoker, cooking meat continuously throughout the day to feed the hungry crowd of people who had gathered here for the moose hunt. Joe had brought some venison he had shot a couple of days earlier near his cabin. Steward also brought food, his always delicious smoked fish. Grey Wolf had also started a large bonfire to keep the men warm while they worked outside the cabin. The family pets were having a reunion they enjoyed once a year, frolicking together, playing in the snow.

After dark, the men sat around the bonfire to keep warm. They decided to take three dogsleds out on the hunt tomorrow, with two men riding on each sled. Black Hawk and Joe would venture off in a different direction to hunt for deer. Johnathan had noticed several deer together in a part of the forest where evergreens were plentiful. They had found this area with an abundance of food and would probably be parking themselves there for the winter. The other four men would head out to search for moose, hoping they would be able to shoot one.

The night was getting late, the men retiring to their assigned sleeping areas. The men whose wives were with them would sleep in the cabin, while the rest took up residence in the shed. The family pets, all spoiled dogs, slept with their owners. The outside fire burned down, extinguishing the last coals before midnight. The night was black with a heavy cloud cover. The men sleeping in the shed stirred, pulling their warm blankets which were tightly wrapped around them up, the dogs sleeping beside them helping to keep them warm.

Jason knocked on the shed door, waking all the participants in the hunt, telling them they needed to get their dogs and sleds ready to leave. The sun was peeking over the horizon, the dark clouds which had dominated the sky last night had moved on. Before the dogs were harnessed, they were fed and watered. Tangled lines and uncooperative dogs kept the men busy for an hour, before they were finally ready to depart.

With the wives waving goodbye, the dog teams left the cabin on their way to hunt for moose and deer. If successful, the meat would provide this large group of fur trappers with at least a subsistence diet of large game meat over the winter. The men pushed off toward their destinations, hoping for a successful day at winning the first prize, an adult bull moose.

CHAPTER SIXTY-TWO

Black Hawk and Joe left the staging area, turning the sled in the direction Johnathan had told them to go. These two were on the hunt for deer, unlike the rest of the men who would be hunting for moose. Johnathan and Grey Wolf were the next to leave, using Johnathan's huskies. Following them were Jason and Steward, who were using Jason's dog team. The day was cold. The bright sun shone down on the barren landscape, causing the snow to glisten, its white coat reflecting sparkles of purity in this untamed land.

Black Hawk and Joe drove the dog team hard to their destination. They soon parked the sled and continued walking on foot to where the deer had congregated for the winter. The men exited the dogsled, securing it until they got back, walking toward the thicket of evergreens in the distance. The men walked quietly. As they drew closer, Joe saw movement among the trees. At that point, they split up, spreading out until they were about one hundred feet apart. The deer, sensing danger, tried to make a break for it and ran directly into the path of Black Hawk and Joe, who were walking with their rifles cocked.

The deer had no chance, and soon two deer lay dead in the blood-soaked snow in front of the hunters. The men walked back to retrieve their sled. They loaded the two does and took them back to Johnathan's cabin for processing. This year's hunt was off to a good start for Black Hawk and Joe.

The two other dogsleds were getting close to their destination, Johnathan, and Jason, who were driving, soon did the same Black Hawk and Joe had done. When the men thought the time was right, they parked the dogsleds to walk into the bush in the search for moose. They donned their snowshoes and secured the dogs. With rifles in hand, they started the mile walk into the marsh.

Moose are receptive to their environment, sensing changes easily. They are generally wary animals, attentive to what is happening around them. As the men approached the wetlands, they split up into two groups. Jason and Steward entered the wetlands directly, while Johnathan and Grey Wolf circled behind the edge of the swamp. If any moose alerted to their presence and tried to escape, they would have the area covered.

Jason and Steward entered the swamp as quietly as possible, as they believed a moose was likely lying down in the tall grass. Steward thought this would have been a good time to have a dog, who could flush the animal out of its lair. The men moved forward, with no sign of any large mammals. The atmosphere in the swamp was tense and quiet.

Suddenly, gunshots broke the silence. Four repetitive shots rang out, echoing across the swamp, followed by sounds of celebration in the distance. Johnathan and Grey Wolf had successfully shot a moose. The animal must have heard Jason and Steward enter the swamp and tried to escape. The moose walked right into an ambush, brought down with bullets in his head and heart. When Jason and Steward reached the dead moose, Grey Wolf and Johnathan were sitting on the giant animal basking in self glory. The moose hunt was a success, but now the hard work would begin.

CHAPTER SIXTY-THREE

The four men looked at the large bull moose and determined butchering this animal would be a huge job. The animal would be partially processed on site, its rack of antlers given to Black Hawk and White Dove, who were the newest members of the extended family, living and trapping in the forest.

Jason and Johnathan walked back to retrieve the dogsleds, while the two other men stayed to work on gutting the moose. Within a short time, the men were back with the dogs and the rest of the tools needed to butcher the animal. They began work, breaking the carcass into quarters. They removed the moose's head with a saw and planned to leave it at the kill site for the scavengers to feast on after they had left.

Two hours later they loaded the first quarter of the moose they had harvested onto a sled. Jason left with the load to take the hind quarter back to Johnathan's cabin. By the time he returned, Johnathan had already left with another quarter of the moose to take home. When both men had returned form their first trip, the sleds would be loaded with the remainder of the moose and taken to the shed at Johnathan's cabin to be processed further.

Black Hawk and Joe had already moved the smaller doe's to the fur shed at Johnathan and Shining Star's home, and had the animals butchered and placed in the freezer before all of the other men returned from their successful moose hunt. Black Hawk had built a fire in the smoker to cook some of the venison, and also gave some meat to White Dove to cook inside the cabin on the woodstove. When the men returned from the moose hunt, the venison was cooked and ready to feed the hungry hunters.

After eating, the monumental work of processing the moose began. The six men worked diligently butchering the large moose, finishing sometime after dark. A pack of wolves lay waiting in the forest, attracted by the smell of blood and meat. The hunters completed their task by lamp light, securing the shed and returning to the cabin. The men who had slept in the shed the previous night would find space on the floor of the cabin, as the shed needed a thorough cleaning in the daylight.

Tomorrow morning, the meat would be divided among the hunters, and they would all return home to their cabins. Arrangements would be made to transport meat for anyone carrying a second passenger home, who did not have enough room on their sled for all their meat. Exhausted after their busy day, the party broke up early and everyone went to bed, having no difficulty falling asleep.

The wolf pack moved into the vacant camp looking for food but found nothing. Disappointed, the wolves moved on, hoping for better luck on their next encounter with a food source. Nature would eventually feed these animals, however they needed to be patient.

CHAPTER SIXTY-FOUR

Johnathan woke everyone involved in the moose hunt at daybreak, as he sensed a change in the weather was coming. Clouds were moving in, along with a cold north wind. All the signs were pointing to a blizzard within the next twenty-four hours. The trappers also recognized the signs of an impending storm, and within one hour the meat was divided equally amongst the men and the sleds were packed and on their way.

The last one to leave was Steward, who stayed to help prepare the dogs and pack the sleds of his fellow hunters. After Steward's departure, a silence fell over Johnathan and Shining Star's cabin. The chaotic three days of the hunt happened only once a year, a joyous occasion for the closeknit group of family and friends. However, the peace and quiet Johnathan and Shining Star enjoyed when everyone had left was priceless.

All the trappers who participated in the hunt at Johnathan and Blossom's cabin made it home before the blizzard struck. The conditions were good for the dogsleds, and everyone made it home in record time. The trappers had pushed their dogs hard, knowing the consequences of not making it to safety before the blizzard struck.

Jason was one of those travellers on the trail to Dawson, certain Wendy would be worried about him. The sled dogs were running hard, with King having difficulty keeping up. King sensed the urgency of the situation and was trying his best to get back to the safety of the house as quickly as possible. Wendy had completed all of the prep work in anticipation of a big storm and was now waiting patiently, but nervously, for Jason and King to return home. The first flakes of snow were falling from the grey sky when Jason, King, and the dogsled pulled in front of the house.

A weeping Wendy grabbed Jason, hugging him tightly. Situations like this made Wendy wonder how she would survive without Jason, who was her best friend and partner. Kuzih appeared to have missed his dog, King, more than he had missed his father. King felt the same way, knocking Kuzih to the ground and smothering him with wet kisses. Jason put his huskies in the yard and fed them. During a blizzard, the sled dogs would allow themselves to be covered in snow, using the white powder as insulation against the storm. The canines will stay under the snow until the storm ends, when they will then get up from the ground, shake themselves off and go about their business.

The storm struck with a fury. The north wind blew with a vengeance, not yet seen this year. All the trappers who lived in the bush were secure in their cabins, the fires burning in their woodstoves keeping them warm. Jason wondered about the donkeys in the barn, but Wendy assured him she had taken care of them before he returned home.

Memories flooded back to Jason and Wendy of their time spent in their small cabin in the bush. The fear of what could happen if things went wrong during a blizzard was always present in their minds; trying to survive the elements was not an easy task in this land called the Yukon.

CHAPTER SIXTY-FIVE

Jason and Wendy were awakened by King, downstairs, barking. Jason pulled himself out of bed and walked to the bedroom window. Streaks of blue sky could be seen as the morning sun broke over the horizon. The blizzard had ended sometime during the night, leaving a foot of fresh snow covering the ground.

Jason headed down the stairs to let King outside. The house was cold, as the stove's last flames had been extinguished hours earlier. Jason relit the woodstove and soon a crackling fire was again sending warmth throughout the house. Jason returned to his bedroom upstairs. Wendy was sleeping comfortably, so Jason decided not to disturb her. He dressed and then returned downstairs, donning the rest of his winter gear so he could go outside.

Jason opened his front door to a winter wonderland, where the new snow covered everything in sight. The evergreen trees, which surrounded the house, wore a fresh coat of white. The morning sun reflected off the white snow, showcasing the beauty nature can create. Many times, such a sight is proven to be merely an illusion of what life is really like living in this northern paradise. Beauty is in the eyes of the beholder, but not in the trapper's vision, who is trying to survive in this wilderness.

Jason checked on the donkeys in the barn. The animals were hungry, but otherwise were doing fine. Jason fed the animals and added some fresh bedding to their pens, while he also checked on the chickens and collected their eggs. He then returned to the house, with King in tow. Jason put a kettle of water on the now hot stove for coffee, while King laid down beside the woodstove, basking in the warmth which radiated from its hot belly.

Going upstairs to wake Wendy, Jason informed her the blizzard was over but there was a foot of new snow covering the ground. Wendy pulled herself out of bed and walked over to the bedroom window to look outside, realizing this was just one of many blizzards which would come to Dawson this winter. Jason went downstairs and removed the boiling water from the top of the woodstove. He made two cups of strong coffee, for himself and his wife.

Wendy joined Jason in the kitchen, telling him as soon as she finished her coffee she would bake some bread in the oven. The couple would eat the hot bread with some of the jam preserves Wendy had made last summer. King's loud snoring was the only sound to disturb the silence in the house. Jason watched Wendy mixing the dough, preparing it to go in the oven.

CHAPTER SIXTY-SIX

Wendy sent Jason to the basement for some preserves. A table against the back wall was filled with jars of these delightful treats, many of these vessels having belonged to Bev. Jason then returned upstairs to retrieve a crying Kuzih, who was hungry after he smelled the bread baking downstairs. He had slept in this morning, after his busy day yesterday. He had helped his mother get the house ready for the blizzard and stayed up past his bedtime enjoying the company of his father.

The sweet, tasty jam was slathered over the hot bread, a sweet breakfast treat his mother prepared for him on special occasions. Wendy suggested they take the dog team out for a run and re-open the fishing holes, which had frozen over while Jason was away. Jason thought that was a good idea, leaving the house and taking King with him. He retrieved his dogs and sled, and within a short time had them ready to go.

After a blizzard, the dog team loved to go for a run in the fresh snow. Their exuberance and energy seemed to increase ten-fold at these times, albeit temporarily. Jason mushed his dog team over to the shed, where he loaded an axe and a shovel. Next stop was the front porch, to pick up Wendy and Kuzih, who were waiting there. The huskies pulled hard on their harnesses, ready to run.

Once his wife and child were safely aboard, Jason mushed his dogs toward the lake. As soon as the sled entered onto the lake's icy surface and the dogs saw the open expanse of snow, they ran hard across the lake, not stopping until they reached the other side. King decided not to run with the sled dogs. He stayed on the shore closest to the house, waiting to see what Jason would do next. Jason mushed his dog team back across the lake, toward the house, stopping at the halfway point.

King, seeing Jason stopped, ran out onto the lake to meet him. Using his axe, Jason quickly and efficiently restored a lifeline to food, the fishing holes. Wendy placed some evergreen boughs on top of the holes, hoping to prevent them from refreezing soon. Wendy and Jason decided to take the dogs to the opposite end of the lake to explore the wetland area. Jason was hoping to find a few rabbits, which would make for an easy dinner. He knew there was a large colony of snowshoe hares which lived there.

When King realized they were not heading back to the house, he grew frustrated by all the movement, deciding to go home and wait for Wendy and Jason's return. The sled entered the swamp, situated at the far southern end of the lake. A large beaver lodge loomed in front of them, and sitting right beside the lodge was a large snowshoe rabbit. Jason picked up his rifle and shot the animal, killing it. He wondered why the rabbit had not tried to run away, concluding that perhaps he thought the lodge structure had prevented him from being seen.

The couple spent fifteen minutes looking for another rabbit, with no success. At that point, they decided to return home. The huskies had burned off their excess energy and paced themselves going back to the house, running at a slow trot. They were soon at the shore closest to home, pulling the sled off the lake.

Wendy, Kuzih, and King, who had been waiting onshore, headed to the house, while Jason put the dogs and sled in their rightful places. He took the rabbit to the shed to be cleaned later, thinking that eating rabbit for dinner would be a nice change from the moose and deer they seemed to have eaten for weeks. Their choice and availability of food was decided by nature, not their desires.

CHAPTER SIXTY-SEVEN

Light snow was floating lazily downward from the sky, the large flakes aimlessly settling on the snow-covered ground. Jason finished making his sled dogs comfortable, the animals happy they had gotten the opportunity to run in the fresh snow. Now tired, they would settle in for a nap.

Jason and King returned to the house, Jason telling Wendy he was going to the shed to clean the rabbit. King, hearing this conversation, decided to accompany Jason in the hopes he would be fed. What was considered undesirable meat for humans, was treated as a delicacy by dogs. King did not even have to beg for these leftovers, as Jason threw a waiting King the unusable pieces of meat as he cleaned the rabbit. King caught the pieces of meat in his mouth, savoring the flavour of the food as he instantly swallowed it.

Once finished with his work, Jason left the shed, only to notice fresh tracks encircling the building. Examining the imprints, he knew exactly what kind of an animal had left them. A wolverine had caught the scent of the rabbit being butchered and had come to the shed to investigate. Finding the door locked and smelling King inside, the wolverine had left the area, sauntering back into the forest.

Jason and King returned to the house, giving Wendy the rabbit to cook on the woodstove. Jason sat down in the sitting area, picking up the book he was reading. The book was titled, *The Call of the North*, written by a new and upcoming Canadian author. Jason found his stories captivating and planned to read his other titles when he could find them. Tired from the day's activities, Jason fell asleep with the book in his hands. Wendy found him in the chair, waking him gently to tell him the rabbit was ready to eat.

Over the early dinner, Wendy and Jason discussed they would soon need to start planning for Christmas, as everyone who had attended the moose hunt at Johnathan's cabin would spend Christmas with them in Dawson. Before Wendy's Aunt Bev had died, she made Wendy promise she would continue the tradition of hosting Christmas in her home. There was an expectation of a large dinner being served and a decorated Christmas tree displayed for everyone to enjoy.

The rest of the afternoon and evening was spent relaxing. Jason continued to read his book while Wendy worked on her knitting. The night was black, the sky was full of dark clouds. A gusty north wind rattled the windows of the house, but sleep was pleasant in the oasis of peace the couple had created for themselves, in this land God had created for just this purpose.

CHAPTER SIXTY-EIGHT

The month of December brought frigid temperatures to Dawson. People tried to stay warm in their ramshackle homes, many with unsafe woodstoves and pipes which created fires. Many homes in Dawson burned to the ground every winter, usually with their owners trapped inside, unable to escape the flames. Thoughts of these residents, who had perished in such fires, haunt the consciousness of the people of Dawson. The worry about being the next to experience this fate was always in the minds of these hapless men and women.

The first rays of sunlight shone through the bedroom window, as Jason pulled himself out of bed and walked downstairs to let King outside. The sled dogs, hearing the activity at the house, let out a loud chorus of barking. Jason returned to his bedroom to get dressed, wanting to go outside to feed his dogs and check on the donkeys in the barn. He let Wendy sleep, covering her with the blanket which had fallen to the floor.

Jason quietly left the house, first walking over to where the sled dogs were. With a chorus of sound, the huskies greeted Jason, knowing they were going to be fed. A sudden barking from King drew Jason's attention away from his dogs. The next sound he heard was a chattering squirrel. He immediately knew King had been up to his favorite pastime, chasing and antagonizing squirrels. The result of the obsession typically ended up with the squirrel in the branches high above, chattering obscenities at the dog below, always a comical scene to watch and listen to.

Jason finished feeding his dogs, then walked to the barn, opening the door to a loud greeting from the donkeys inside. Jason spent thirty minutes with the animals, enjoying the love he felt for the donkeys. He fed them hay and gave them fresh water before returning to the house. Upon entering the house, Jason was surprised to see Wendy working in the kitchen. The water in the kettle on the woodstove was already boiling and the smell of frying venison ignited the hunger in Jason's belly. King also noticed the odor of the frying meat, barking outside the front door wanting to be let inside.

Kuzih joined his parents in the kitchen for breakfast, while King was fed and went to lie by the woodstove. A loud knock at the front door startled the couple, with Jason going to see who the visitor was. After the men identified themselves, Jason opened the door to two of the constables who worked out of the North West Mounted Police office in Dawson.

Jason invited them in, and they shared they had been out on patrol when the opportunity to shoot two doe arose. They had encountered the animals just outside of town, only twenty minutes into the bush. They shot the deer, loaded them on their sled and headed back to town. They told Jason the deer would help feed the hungry people in Dawson at Christmas, but the freezers at the Mountie station were full. Jason told the Mounties he had plenty of room and would gladly take the deer from them.

Jason asked the men to leave the deer outside the door of the shed and he would take care of butchering them and storing the meat until Christmas. Wendy would help Jason with this task, as her butchering skills could rival those of any man living in this wilderness. The constables left, thanking the couple and continued their patrol into the forest.

CHAPTER SIXTY-NINE

The day had turned out to be sunny and unusually warm for December. Jason suggested to Wendy he would quickly gut the deer and place them inside the shed. They would keep safely there until tomorrow when they would work together to butcher them. Today, he said he would get the dog team ready and they could bundle up Kuzih in the bearskin blanket and head out on the lake to do some fishing. They were ready to leave the house well before noon.

King decided to accompany his family on this trip and followed closely behind the sled. After a short run across the lake, the couple reached the area they were going to fish. Jason removed the snow from the holes and the cedar broughs Wendy had placed there. Jason cleared the holes of any new ice which had formed since their last visit. Soon, Wendy was placing her nets under the ice, letting the current do its job catching the fish.

After two hours on the ice, the couple gathered up their catch and returned to their warm house. Most of the fish were stored in the outside freezer to be cleaned later. The sled dogs had been rewarded with fresh whitefish while at the lake, and Jason reserved a large lake trout to clean and eat for lunch. Jason left the dogsled intact, as they were planning to take Kuzih out later to complete a Christmas tradition, cutting a fresh tree for the house,

Wendy went inside with Kuzih to stoke the fire and warm up, while King followed Jason to the shed to help him clean the trout. He loved assisting with this job, as there were always some kind of treat in store for him. After a delicious meal of fresh fish, the couple took Kuzih upstairs where they would all take a short nap. After waking, they would head out with the dog team to find a Christmas tree.

A gentle breeze rippled across the land, the serenity of the moment catching the attention of the couple who had just woken from their nap. They roused Kuzih, as they wanted to find a suitable Christmas tree before dark. Once they were all bundled up again, Jason guided the dog team to a forested area a short distance from their house. He was sure this area had trees the size they needed for their living room. Kuzih got to pick the tree, but only if his parents agreed with his choice.

After thirty minutes of searching through the evergreens, the family decided on the perfect tree, even getting a bark of approval from King. Jason cut the tree and loaded it onto the sled. They travelled back to the house and prepared an area in the living room, where the tree would stand. The beautiful tree, with its aromatic evergreen smell permeating the living room, was now ready to be decorated. The spirit of Christmas would soon capture the hearts of the friends and family who would be joining Wendy, Jason, and Kuzih here at Christmastime.

CHAPTER SEVENTY

Bev stored her Christmas decorations on the bottom floor of the house, because she lived alone. After she died, and Jason and Wendy moved into the house, the couple moved the decorations from the ground floor to the attic to save space in their living area. The couple planned to retrieve the decorations from the attic and finish looking through the boxes they had previously discovered there. Kuzih, being an inquisitive child, would be a willing participant in this venture.

With Wendy's help, Jason pulled the dresser beneath the attic opening and hoisted himself up through the trap door in the ceiling. He then reached for Kuzih, pulling him from Wendy's arms and setting him on the floor beside him. Jason pulled his wife up through the opening, leaving only King on the floor below.

Jason lit the lantern which had been left in the attic for this purpose, to throw some light into the dark interior of the room. A dull light shone through the small window which graced the front of the attic. As they looked around, Wendy was curious about an old trunk covered in dust, which sat in the corner of the room. She dusted off the top of the trunk and carefully opened it. Brilliantly coloured vintage Indigenous clothing immediately caught her eye. The clothing was from Bev's childhood and teen years, items that she had treasured and packed in the trunk for safekeeping. Examining the beautiful, hand-made, embroidered clothing Wendy admired the craftsmanship, realizing the hard work which had gone into each piece. She gently refolded each garment and returned them to their original place, closing the lid.

The afternoon was passing quickly, and Kuzih was anxious to decorate the Christmas tree after dinner. The couple gathered up the boxes of decorations and Wendy climbed down to the dresser below. Jason handed the decorations down to his wife, who placed the boxes on the floor beside her. Jason then handed Kuzih down and lowered himself, pulling the trap door back over the hole they had climbed through.

Wendy cooked a stew for dinner, using moose meat and some of the vegetables she had stored in the basement from last fall's garden harvest. These included carrots, potatoes, and turnips, of which she had an abundance. After dinner Jason and Wendy cleaned up the kitchen while Kuzih waited patiently for them in the living room.

The couple soon joined their son, spending a joyous time placing the decorations on the tree. Old ornaments, passed down through the years, were now family heirlooms adorning their tree. Christmas was, and always will be, a time of special celebration in this family's Dawson home in Canada's Yukon.

CHAPTER SEVENTY-ONE

The guests were arriving from their cabins in the bush. Wendy and Jason welcomed their extended family for the annual Christmas celebration which had been hosted by Bev over the past years for this isolated community in the forest. Wendy and Jason were now responsible for carrying on this yearly tradition at Christmas.

The guest list for dinner read as follows: Johnathan and Shining Star, with their son Grey Eagle, were the first to arrive. They were followed by Steward and Blossom, long time residents of the forest community. Joe and Mary were attending with Rusty, their only canine. Grey Wolf and Rose had met Black Hawk and White Dove on the trail travelling here. They finished their journey together, the last to arrive at Jason and Wendy's home in Dawson.

A sense of sorrow greeted these people as they gathered as family, memories of Bev dominating their thoughts. The Yukon was not the same without this stalwart of the north, who now joined the group in spirit only.

A cold north wind blew the snow across the deserted streets of Dawson. Smoke billowing from the chimneys of the homes were the only visible signs of life. As the bright sun shone down on this frozen land, the silence of the moment was a reflection of life here. This was a land God created, and then forgot, a land they called the Yukon.

BLACK HAWK AND WHITE DOVE

CHAPTER ONE

The snow had arrived in the Yukon in November, covering the land in a blanket of white. Black Hawk and White Dove sat in their cabin, with their dog, Nicky. The heat created by the wood burning in the stove sent warm air radiating throughout their home. A steady column of grey smoke spewed from the chimney, disappearing into the cloud-filled sky above.

Suddenly Nicky's ears perked up, the dog had heard something. Moments later, the couple heard the distant sound of dogs barking. Black Hawk opened the front door of their cabin and looked outside. Travelling across the lake, in the direction of their cabin, were two dogsleds. The men mushing the sleds were Black Hawk's father, Bear Claw, and his uncle, Broken Arrow. Black Hawk's father was delivering the dog team he had promised his son.

Within a half hour, the sleds pulled up in front of the wilderness cabin. Bear Claw reached out for his son and daughter-in-law, hugging both tightly. White Dove had placed a kettle of water on the hot cooktop of the stove to make coffee they had been gifted yesterday. Two Mounties from Dawson, on a routine patrol checking wilderness cabins, had stopped in just the day before. After passing an inspection and wellness check by the Mounties, the couple had been gifted coffee and sugar, with a farewell wish for a safe and merry Christmas. White Dove was pleased she could now offer the hot beverage to her visiting family.

The group retreated into the warm cabin, thankful for the hot coffee. After resting, the men got to work unloading the sleds. Broken Arrow's sled was loaded with supplies donated by the tribe to help the young couple get through their first winter alone in the bush. Bear Claw had carried with him twenty pounds of moose meat and a similar amount of venison for the young couple. Black Hawk and White Dove had been subsisting on rabbits and grouse, making the venison and moose a delicious change of taste.

The men put the supplies in their rightful places and then got Black Hawk's new dog team settled in the yard he had ready for them. They fed and watered the animals, hoping the huskies would adapt well to their pristine environment, living at the cabin. White Dove extended an invitation to Black Hawk's father and uncle, asking them to spend the night. She had taken venison and left it near the woodstove to thaw, planning to cook the meat for dinner.

Returning to the cabin, the men enjoyed spending time together, discussing everyone back home. Black Hawk told his father about the moose hunt he had been invited to participate in. He told his father he had delivered the dog team at just the right time, as he could now join the hunt and if it was a success, use his dogsled to bring a load of meat home. White Dove cooked the venison, sending everyone, including Nicky, to sleep with a full stomach. Bear Claw told his son he was pleased to finally see where the couple were living and was glad they had made out so well.

Bear Claw and his brother left early the following morning. The group embraced, saying goodbye, and wishing each other good luck. Quiet settled over the cabin when their company left, making Black Hawk and White Dove feel a bit lonely. However, they were happy to be living on their own in the bush, relying on one another. Black Hawk and White Dove went outside to check on their new dog team. With the addition of the dogs his father gave them, their chances of surviving the winter was assured, not a given in this land which offers few friendly gestures.

CHAPTER TWO

The morning sun was slowly rising above the treeline when Black Hawk opened the cabin door to let Nicky outside. The wind-swept snow blew across the frozen lake in front of the cabin. White Dove watched from the window as a pack of wolves chased a deer onto the lake. The deer, slowed down by the deep snow, became an easy victim for the more agile wolves. They easily caught the doe, taking it down and killing it by ripping out the hapless animal's throat. The pack of wolves then converged on the body, ready to eat their kill. The wolves would leave little food when finished eating, even the scavengers which hung around until the wolves were finished would not find enough leftovers for a meal.

Black Hawk's new team of huskies had attracted this wolf pack to their cabin, curious as to who had invaded their territory. There was no love lost between huskies and wolves, who considered each other archenemies. Fierce battles between these canines typically ended in the death of one or the other of the animals.

Black Hawk told White Dove they would use the dog team today to see how the huskies would respond to their new owners. The day was sunny, with little breeze, a perfect day to run the dogs on the lake. The lakes in the Yukon had frozen early this year, as brutal cold from the north had arrived two weeks earlier than expected.

Black Hawk ventured outside to feed his huskies, giving each of his dogs a big loving hug. The happy dogs loved Black Hawk, a few of them pushing him on his back and giving him big wet kisses. Black Hawk realized the dogs were young and still liked to play. As these young dogs grow into adults, they will become hardened and wise in the ways to survive in this brutal environment. Black Hawk had prior experience with dogs, having helped his father with dogsleds since he was a small boy. If treated with respect and well-fed, a bond will be established between the musher and his team, making the dogs work hard for their owner.

Soon the couple were running their new dog team on the lake. They had left Nicky, their pet, at home in the cabin, afraid she would not be able to keep up with the enthusiastic young dog team which was now part of her family. Black Hawk and White Dove mushed the dogs to the site on the lake where they had watched the wolves kill the deer. Upon arrival, remnants of fur, skin, bones, and a large area of bright red snow, attested to the fact a large animal had been killed and eaten here. The occasional raven was still landing at the site, hopping around, and looking for anything edible left behind.

Black Hawk let the huskies run for thirty more minutes, before taking them back to the cabin. Once home, the couple returned the huskies to their yard, while they retired to the cabin. White Dove put a kettle of water on the woodstove to make coffee. While waiting for it to boil, the couple discussed the moose hunt at Johnathan and Shining Star's cabin. They were to leave in three days, glad the dogsled would make it a short trip of less than two hours.

That evening, while enjoying dinner, the winds started blowing loudly through trees surrounding the couple's cabin. No snow accompanied the windstorm which blew hard all night, causing the tree trunks and limbs to creak and groan. The following morning, the sun appeared over the horizon, promising sunshine for another day.

CHAPTER THREE

Black Hawk and White Dove were going to work in their fur shed this morning. They planned to organize the building, making room for the supplies Black Hawk's father and uncle had brought them. Valuable items were included in this gift, meant to help them start their new life in the bush. There were snowshoes, an extra dog harness, and warm blankets. The couple were each gifted a pair of winter mitts, made by an elder in their tribe whose specialty was turning fur into warm winter wear. The couple would use the mitts when travelling to Johnathan's cabin tomorrow morning.

Black Hawk was pleased to see his father had included new traps, including a beaver trap, in his gift. After returning from the moose hunt, the couple planned to run a small trapline for the first three weeks of December. As they were planning to travel to Dawson for the Christmas celebration at Wendy and Jason's home, they would wait to establish a longer trapline until the first of the year.

The couple spent the rest of the day getting ready to leave on their trip. Black Hawk set rabbit snares in the afternoon, hoping to catch some food to take with them.

They wanted the venison and moose meat Bear Claw had gifted them to remain in their outdoor freezer, in case the moose hunt was a bust. Spending their first winter at their new home, the couple were apprehensive about having enough food to survive.

Cloud cover filled the morning sky as Black Hawk woke his wife, telling her he was preparing the dogsled and then going to check the rabbit snares. He told White Dove he would be returning shortly, hopefully with fresh meat. The dogs were ready for an adventure, trying to help Black Hawk put their harnesses on. Once he managed to get the dogs hooked up to the sled, the man and his dogs set out to check the snares. The traps proved productive, Black Hawk collecting six large rabbits which lay dead on the frozen ground. Retrieving this food source, they returned to the cabin, where White Dove and Nicky were waiting.

The couple loaded their personal belongings on the sled and were soon ready to leave for Johnathan and Shining Star's cabin. Black Hawk secured the door to the cabin and yelled for Nicky to come. He gave the command for his team to start, and they headed down the trail. If the moose hunt was successful, they would return with an ample supply of meat for their outdoor freezer. This was the result the young couple prayed for, food to keep them alive this winter

CHAPTER FOUR

Black Hawk mushed his dog team toward the forest trail which led to Johnathan and Shining Star's cabin. The clouds had dissipated, and the sun shone down on the happy couple and their dog, Nicky, as the huskies pulled the sled through the soft snow. Pristine silence enveloped the senses of the couple, only the loud breathing from the sled dogs broke the quiet of the moment. The sun's rays shone down on the white snow, reflecting a million tiny lights, revealing the beauty of nature's hand.

The huskies pulled hard on their harnesses, their hot breath leaving a trail of steam among the trees in the forest. Meeting another dogsled on the trail was not what Black Hawk expected, when Grey Wolf and Rose, travelling to the same destination, crossed his path. Black Hawk and White Dove had never met these strangers, but after realizing they were going to the same destination, they introduced themselves. Grey Wolf and Rose lived much closer to Dawson and had left their home at sunrise. They were just a few years older than Black Hawk and White Dove and had heard about the newcomers in the bush from Wendy, Rose's cousin. The two couples decided to travel together the rest of the way to Johnathan and Shining Star's.

After another hour of travel, the two sleds arrived at their hosts' cabin, where a team of sled dogs and a single dogsled graced the front yard. Loud conversations and constant movement in and out of the cabin greeted the couples upon their arrival. Black Hawk and Grey Wolf parked and secured their dogsleds closer to an outbuilding, which was a short distance away from the house. Too many dogs in a small area can create anxiety among the animals, which can lead to disagreements and physical fights.

The couples exited their sleds and walked toward Johnathan's cabin. Grey Wolf and Rose introduced Black Hawk and White Dove to their fellow trappers and families at the cabin who they had not yet met. Johnathan and Shining Star were happy to see the new arrivals and pleased Black Hawk and White Dove had decided to join their group.

The men in attendance cooked venison and Black Hawk's rabbit in the smoker, while the women were busy cooking food on the woodstove inside the cabin. The hunt would begin tomorrow morning, and as the men sat around the outdoor fire, they planned their strategy. Black Hawk and Joe, another member of the clan, were paired together and directed to an area where the prospect of shooting a deer was good. The other four men would go in a different direction to hunt moose.

After an evening of overeating and robust conversation, the crowd finally settled down and found their assigned sleeping areas. The following morning came early. Black Hawk's dogsled was the first to leave, with Joe on board. Excitement mounted as the two men thought of shooting a deer, their senses on high alert.

CHAPTER FIVE

The day was sunny and cold, causing the dog team to run fast toward their destination. The huskies loved to run in the sunshine, feeling the warmth of its rays on their back made the dogs happy in spirit. The deer hunters' plans were to leave their sled a thirty minute walk from where their prey was located, so as not to spook them. The deer were living in a large stand of evergreen trees, which provided them with food and shelter.

Reaching their destination, Black Hawk and Joe exited the sled, donned snowshoes, and started walking toward the evergreens in the distance. The men had decided to split up, with Joe heading toward where the thicket ended. Black Hawk would walk into the middle of the evergreens, hoping to scare the animals toward Joe. Their plan was not executed fully, because as soon as they separated, two doe came out from their cover and were immediately shot by Joe and Black Hawk.

Jubilation at their success was evident, as a smiling Black Hawk went to retrieve the dogsled, while a grinning Joe began to field dress the deer. Once the dog team arrived, the men were ready to load the deer and take them back to

Johnathan's cabin to be butchered. The return trip to the cabin was fast, and soon the doe were hung and ready to be processed. The men hunting moose were not expected back until late afternoon, giving Joe and Black Hawk time to use the shed to butcher the deer.

Four hours later, the men finished, and the venison was packed away. The meat would be divided between the families when they were ready to return home. In the afternoon, the moose hunters returned to Johnathan's cabin, also successful with their hunt. The men had shot a bull moose and delivered the animal, cut in quarters, to the fur shed. Black Hawk and White Dove were presented with the antlers from the moose, as they were the newest members of this close-knit forest community, made up of friends and family. Black Hawk planned to display the antlers proudly above the front door of his cabin.

The following morning, with the threat of severe weather headed their way, the hunters and their families left Johnathan and Shining Star's cabin with enough meat to last each of them through the winter. Black Hawk would return for his share of the meat later, as there was little room for it on the sled with White Dove and the moose antlers. Johnathan had plenty of space to store the meat until the weather improved. Black Hawk felt lucky Johnathan lived so close, making a return trip easy.

The dogsleds left intermittently, until Steward was the only one left to say goodbye. Johnathan and Shining Star's once chaotic cabin became peaceful again, leaving the couple to enjoy the serenity of nature which surrounded them.

The trip home for Black Hawk and White Dove was

uneventful. White Dove carried the large rack of moose antlers on her lap while Black Hawk mushed the dogs. Nicky did well running beside the sled as it maneuvered its way down the forest trail. Less than two hours later, they were pulling up to their cabin. Black Hawk removed the nails he had used to secure the door before leaving for the moose hunt, allowing White Dove and Nicky to enter their home.

White Dove started a fire in the woodstove to warm the cabin and to boil water for coffee. Black Hawk returned the sled dogs to the yard, ensuring they were all fed well before the snows began. Shortly thereafter, White Dove heard a banging sound outside the cabin's front door. She opened the door to find a smiling Black Hawk, proudly looking at the moose antlers he had placed above the cabin door. His father would be proud of him, Black Hawk wishing they could cherish this moment together.

CHAPTER SIX

The slow-moving blizzard settled over the Yukon with an unforgiving fury. A weather system had blocked the storm's forward progress, slowing it to a crawl. This allowed the moose hunters and their families, who lived in wilderness cabins deep in the forest and relied on fur trapping for survival, time to arrive safely back to their cabins and prepare themselves for the blizzard. Jason was the only participant who owned a house in Dawson, which meant he had the furthest to travel. Luckily, he also managed to make it home before the storm hit hard.

Black Hawk and White Dove had carried a package of venison home from Johnathan and Shining Star's cabin, leaving the rest of their meat to be picked up after the blizzard was over and the skies were clear and sunny once more. Late afternoon saw an increase in the wind speed, with heavy snow filling the darkened sky. The glass in the windows of the cabin rattled each time a gust of wind buffeted the building. Nicky slept comfortably by the woodstove, the storm outside was nothing the dog was concerned with, as she was safe and warm in the cabin.

The blizzard raged through the night, keeping a nervous

Black Hawk and his wife on high alert. As the first light of dawn broke over the horizon, the winds began to subside, signaling the storm was over. Jason pulled himself out from under the warm covers of the bed and looked out the window. The sun, looking like a fiery red ball, was slowly rising over the tree line at the end of the lake. A veil of pure white snow covered the outside world.

Watching from his bedroom window, Black Hawk spotted a fox in the front of the cabin. The animal, unaware anyone was watching, acted without fear. He played in the deep snow, hopping like a rabbit across the couple's yard. Stillness descended over the forest which surrounded the cabin, when a lone raven appeared in an endless blue sky. He was trying to find his fellow brethren, who he had become separated from during the storm. The raven's shrill cry pierced the morning air, as the bird flew over the area looking for his lost mates.

A bark from Nicky spurred Black Hawk into action, walking to the front door to let Nicky outside. He then dressed, to follow his dog, wanting to check his sled dogs who had been out all night in the storm. Black Hawk knew feeding the dogs and talking to them would bring them comfort, letting the dogs know they were safe. While feeding the excited canines, Black Hawk thought he might take the dogs for a run on the lake later this afternoon. White Dove had suggested taking the nets and fishing under the ice when the storm abated, and it was the perfect day to do so. Sunny skies were above them, with the air as calm as it could be.

Suddenly, Nicky began barking loudly, pulling Black Hawk's attention away from his dog team. Scanning the lake, Black Hawk could see a spray of snow being thrown up behind sled dogs, as a team pulled a sled through the snow. The man driving the sled saw Black Hawk and the smoke from his chimney drifting over the frozen lake. He altered his course, steering his dogs toward Black Hawk and White Dove's cabin.

CHAPTER SEVEN

When the sled arrived at their cabin, Nicky liked the man immediately. The dog acted as if this man was a long-lost friend. Gerald was a large man with a barrel chest, who shouted out a greeting to Black Hawk, asking him how they had fared in the storm. Black Hawk found Gerald to be friendly and invited him inside.

Seated at the table, drinking a cup of fresh brewed coffee, Gerald asked Black Hawk and White Dove how they would feel about having him and his wife, Beth, as their new neighbours. Gerald was one of the few lucky men who had made a fortune during the Alaska gold rush, after moving on from the Klondike a year or so ago. He had returned to Dawson with his newfound wealth, buying a small home in town which came with a dog team. Gerald told Black Hawk and White Dove his wife was in New York City, and he was sending for her this spring.

The couple had lived in New York before Gerald left the city and travelled to the Klondike looking for gold. He had left his wife behind to live with her parents, and although he now had the little house in Dawson, he had recently purchased an old fur trapper's cabin and land on the lake.

He planned to build a new cabin for he and his wife to live in, turning the old house into a storage shed. Gerald had not seen his wife in almost three years but hoped by using hired labor from town and buying lumber from a local sawmill, run by a man named Tim, he could have the new home ready for her by next fall.

White Dove asked Gerald where Beth was going to stay while he built the new cabin he promised her on the lake. Gerald told the couple if the house in Dawson did not meet with her approval, he would rent a room at the finest hotel money could buy until their new home was ready. Black Hawk and White Dove realized this man's dreams were hopeless, but wished him well with this endeavour. Gerald was envisioning a new life with his wife, surrounded by nature. However, the couple did not believe living with beavers and muskrats would make Beth a happy woman.

Finishing their coffee, Gerald said he should be heading home but was happy to have met his new neighbors. After his sled had pulled onto the lake, the couple laughed hysterically at the thought of the encounter Gerald would have with his wife, when she realized the hardships she would be facing living in the bush. A divorce for Gerald and life alone in the remote wilds of the Yukon were the probable outcomes of his plan. Black Hawk and White Dove thought Gerald's idea would fall by the wayside, and they would never meet Beth. But Gerald would not change his plans, believing his love missed him and would join him here under any circumstances, good or bad.

The couple got ready to take the dogsled out on the lake to fish for whitefish. This protein was needed to feed their team of huskies. The dogs needed to be strong and healthy to perform their required tasks, which would keep these young fur trappers alive.

CHAPTER EIGHT

As the dogsled slid over the snow with grace, Black Hawk and White Dove loved the feeling of the chilly air blowing across their faces. The lake was frozen to a depth which made traveling anywhere on its surface a safe venture. Black Hawk let the dogs run, knowing this was what the huskies liked to do best. He eventually steered the dogs around the lake, ending their run at the holes in the ice used for fishing.

Black Hawk took his axe and broke the ice which had reformed over the openings he had created earlier. The couple placed their net through the hole, letting the current guide it to where the whitefish and lake trout congregated. Allowing the net to float aimlessly for a brief time, it was pulled back up to the top of the ice. Repeating this procedure a half a dozen times, enough fish were caught to feed the dogs and themselves for three days. Black Hawk and White Dove would work together cleaning the lake trout after loading the dogsled and returning to the cabin.

Pulling the sled onto the shoreline, the couple were met by Nicky, their family pet. The dog was jumping around, excited at smelling the fish on the sled, her mouth salivating at the thought of eating dinner. White Dove went to the cabin to add wood to the dying fire, while Black Hawk unloaded the sled, placing the fish in the fur shed.

Black Hawk placed his sled dogs in their yard and retrieved one whitefish from the shed for each of them. This was dinner for his work dogs tonight. He also fed Nicky a small whitefish before returning to the fur shed to clean the trout. With White Dove's help, the lake trout were cleaned, with some fish being placed in their outdoor freezer and the rest going to be cooked for tonight's dinner. The couple headed back to the house, happy with their productive excursion on the lake. Once inside, Nicky whined to be let out. When Black Hawk went to open the door, he told his wife he had forgotten to do something at the fur shed and would be right back.

He left to do something his wife knew nothing about. An annoying wolverine had become a common sight around the cabin in recent days, always hoping to come up with a free meal. Black Hawk had been feeding the wolverine and the animal was starting to trust him. If White Dove knew her husband was doing this, she would tell Black Hawk to kill the wolverine, which she considered evil and bad luck. Black Hawk thought otherwise, finding this animal's behaviour fascinating and its commitment to its surroundings profound.

Black Hawk would soon tell White Dove about befriending the wolverine, with the promise to shoot it and process its fur after their trapping season started. He would double cross this predator, who would do likewise if ever given the chance. This was the way of the Yukon, where sometimes life did not matter, unless it was your own.

CHAPTER NINE

The tantalizing smell of lake trout sizzling in the frying pan on the hot cooktop of the woodstove whetted the appetites of the residents in the cabin. Nicky, who felt she had not eaten anything substantial in two days despite just finishing a whitefish, was waiting patiently for food. White Dove fed Nicky first and then joined her husband at the table to eat the succulent fillets she had prepared for dinner.

The couple talked about running a small trapline for the month of December. In two days, they would set out ten traps and work that line until the end of the third week of December. Then, the traps would be retrieved and stored until they returned from their trip to Dawson. Wendy and Jason had invited Black Hawk and White Dove to join the forest community in a celebration of Christmas, which the young couple had agreed to attend. Nicky would love joining this annual event, where she would get to see the canine friends she had met at the moose hunt.

The sky was darkening and a strong north wind had picked up. After finishing dinner, Black Hawk took Nicky outside. He looked at the menacing clouds which had been blown into the area by the increasing wind. The treetops in the forest surrounding him swayed from side to side, groaning. When Nicky finished her business, Black Hawk called her to go back inside. He then grabbed meat from the outdoor freezer, before joining his wife. White Dove, sensing the urgency from her husband, carried extra firewood inside to get ready for the oncoming storm.

The couple secured the cabin, their small home in this hostile land was the only thing they could depend on for their survival during dangerous blizzards which swept across the region at this time of year. The fierce wind howled outside the cabin. As it blew through the bare limbs of the deciduous trees which surrounded their property, the moaning from the tree trunks rubbing against one another sent an unsettling sound throughout the forest. The storm lasted until the first streaks of a red sky could be seen through the cabin window at dawn.

Black Hawk pulled himself out of bed and looked outside at a winter scene witnessed by few. It was a special gift from nature to the hardy men and women who spent their lives in this beautiful, but inhospitable, land. Black Hawk dressed, wanting to let Nicky out and check on his sled dogs, anxious as to how they had fared during the storm.

CHAPTER TEN

When let outside, Nicky jumped and played in the fresh powdered snow like a child. Black Hawk's huskies were glad to see him but were hungry. He retrieved enough whitefish from the outdoor freezer to give one fish to each of his dogs for breakfast. The huskies loved to receive the fish frozen, and would consume every part of it, leaving nothing for any scavengers. Typically, ravens would gather around the property at feeding time, always hopeful of a few tidbits being left for them. Black Hawk headed to the fur shed to light a fire in the woodstove, planning to work there later in the morning.

Black Hawk returned to the cabin with Nicky, where he was overwhelmed by the aroma of venison frying on the woodstove. Over breakfast, Black Hawk suggested to his wife they get the traps ready for the trapline. They could then take the dog team and scout the area more thoroughly, looking for signs of fur bearing mammals.

After finishing breakfast, Black Hawk and White Dove went to the shed to sort out their traps. They selected the ones they planned to use, placing them in a large iron pot of water to boil. This would ensure no smell of humans would deter animals from being attracted to the bait and caught. Black Hawk then ventured outside to harness the dog team, his wife joining him on the sled when they were ready to leave.

Nicky was staying home today, left to guard the cabin. The day was sunny, and the winds had calmed to a light breeze. The dogs happily pulled the sled through the fresh white snow, breaking the trail. Black Hawk followed the well-worn path the former fur trapper, Johnathan, had previously used while living in the cabin. The couple noticed fresh signs of small mammals, such as martens and weasels, but no tracks for any larger animals. Black Hawk told his wife these observations did not mean much, as the majority of the animals were still safely tucked away wherever they had weathered the storm.

The couple headed home, happy with the outcome of their trip into the bush. Upon their return, they were surprised to see a dogsled sitting in their front yard. It was Steward, who shouted and waved, greeting the returning couple. Black Hawk and White Dove were pleased to have company, something which rarely happened, especially in the winter.

Steward helped Black Hawk return the sled dogs to their yard, and then they walked back to the cabin, where White Dove was boiling water for coffee. Steward explained the reason for his visit, telling Black Hawk he had noticed what a fine team of young huskies his father had gifted him while they were on the moose hunt. Steward would like one of his female huskies, who was now in heat, to breed with Black Hawk's alpha male, the lead dog. He told Black Hawk

After the Gold Rush 225

and White Dove when the puppies were born, they would be able to choose their pick of the litter. The couple agreed, knowing how much happiness a puppy would add to their often-mundane lives.

The men went outside, where Steward unhooked the lucky lady from her harness. Black Hawk retrieved his alpha male, Chief, from the yard. When the dog realized why he was taken from his kennel, a primeval instinct captured him. Chief knew what his job was, and he finished it with pleasure. Because of Chief's masculinity and strength, his species would survive another day.

Steward returned his now impregnated female husky back to her place on his team. He left with little fanfare, for his short journey home. He told Black Hawk and White Dove, he and Blossom would see them at Wendy and Jason's house for Christmas, an event everyone was looking forward to.

Steward was pleased Black Hawk and White Dove had agreed to breed the dogs. He currently had no dogs for sale, anxious to have this batch of puppies, with Chief being the father. Trades were a convenient bargaining tool in this land where people possessed little to no money. It was a savage place where only friendships and trust worked to keep one alive, a land intent on trying to do one harm.

CHAPTER ELEVEN

Black Hawk and White Dove awoke to an overcast sky. Nature would provide no sunshine today for the couple, who planned to set ten steel traps and six rabbit snares on their trapline. Rabbits were harvested easily with snares set in their runways made in the deep snow. Like a roadway, these trails snake through the bush, making it easier for the animals to move around in their habitat. The runways help the rabbits escape predators, as the prey does not get trapped in the deep snow while trying to run away.

Unfortunately for the hares, they cannot escape the predator known as man, who crafts his wire into a loop and places it into their highways. The snare wire is secured to a strong lower branch of a tree, which will keep the rabbits from escaping. The rabbits do not see these death traps, unable to avoid them as they peacefully lumber down the trails. When a rabbit or hare meets the wire, it wraps around its neck. As the hapless animal tries to escape, the wire tightens and strangles it, resulting in the animal's death.

Black Hawk let Nicky outside. She would not be accompanying Black Hawk and White Dove today as they set their trapline. The couple skipped breakfast, thinking they would eat when they returned home. Black Hawk retrieved the excited sled dogs, who sensed they were going on a run this morning. After hooking up their harnesses, the dogs pulled the sled over to the fur shed where White Dove was waiting. The couple loaded the animal traps, adding an axe to the sled to cut a hole in the ice to set the one beaver trap they owned.

As Black Hawk mushed his dog team, the sled shot forward through the combined effort of the dogs running in unison down the forest trail. A short ride on the dogsled brought the fur trappers to their first stop. Black Hawk was an experienced trapper, his father having taught him the ways of the mammals he was trapping for fur. Black Hawk felt he belonged to the forest which surrounded him. The couple spent the morning selecting locations to set their traps and snares, hoping they had chosen their placement well.

The beaver trap was the last one the couple would set. Black Hawk mushed his dogs onto the frozen beaver pond. Selecting a spot close to the lodge, he cut a hole in the ice with his axe and lowered the trap into the hole. Catching a beaver was double the prize for these early trappers, as it was both a valuable pelt and a food source, enjoyed by almost all. The meat made a delicious stew and saved many a trapper from starvation.

CHAPTER TWELVE

After finishing setting the beaver trap, the couple took an exploratory trip around the wetlands. The frozen swamp was quiet, with the only noise being the occasional drumbeat of a woodpecker's beak against the dry wood of a dead tree. Throughout this ecosystem, Black Hawk counted five beaver lodges. A healthy population of muskrats also lived here with the beavers; their homes located everywhere in the frozen swamp.

Suddenly, a loud gunshot broke the silence. Black Hawk and White Dove froze in disbelief. Black Hawk discharged his rifle, to let whoever had fired the shot know he had company nearby. Ten minutes later, a dogsled came into view, with the man waving in greeting. The stranger was an Indigenous hunter, looking for food to feed his family. He told Black Hawk and White Dove the gunshot they had heard was him shooting a deer, which lay dead a short distance from here. The man kindly offered to share the meat with the couple, which they declined telling the hunter they had a good supply in their freezer. The man returned to his kill site to butcher the deer; he would return to his family a happy man.

Black Hawk and White Dove headed home, glad to be finished with their day working the trapline. White Dove entered the cabin to a waiting Nicky, who was cold because the fire in the woodstove was out. Suddenly, she heard a gunshot ring out. She raced to the cabin door, opened it, and looked outside. Black Hawk walked from around the corner of the cabin, carrying a dead wolverine. He had lured the unsuspecting animal into a death trap by offering him food. He had informed his wife of his secret while setting traps this morning. After stating her displeasure about the situation, White Dove was happy her husband had chosen to kill this animal, which she considered a bad omen to have around their cabin.

White Dove jokingly told Black Hawk, to his dismay, the wolverine would be the first fur they harvested this season. She told him to take the animal to the fur shed to prepare his pelt for tanning. The wolverine's remains would be used to bait any traps which needed to be refurbished tomorrow. Black Hawk sadly went to the fur shed to do what his wife asked of him. The wolverine he was now going to butcher was like a pet he had betrayed. He had named this solitary animal, with few allies in the forest, Friendly. He cried as he pulled the hide from the dead animal, having considered Friendly a friend, not a foe.

Black Hawk left the fur shed with Friendly's hide stretched across a board. He returned to the cabin, where he found his wife preparing something to eat. The couple had eaten no breakfast, so hunger gnawed in their bellies. White Dove was frying steak on the woodstove, with Nicky already hanging out around the couple's dining table, waiting for food. Black Hawk ate his meal in silence, White Dove having no pity on him. She knew how he felt about killing what is usually a fur trapper's biggest enemy, the wolverine, but thought he had been foolish to ever befriend him.

The December nights were long when living in a cabin in the wilds of Canada's Yukon. It was a way of life reserved for only a few. The loneliness and seclusion was relished, but only if madness from the isolation did not take over one's mind, sending him into the forest to die and join the many souls who suffered the same fate. This would be an end to a dream no one wished for.

CHAPTER THIRTEEN

The wolf pack circled the cabin; the sled dogs, sensing their presence, barked out a loud warning. Nicky, sleeping by the woodstove, awakened from her sleep. She growled at the wolves' scent, which had invaded her nostrils. The wolf pack became more brazen, accosting the huskies. The dogs, being restrained, had no chance of winning a fight if the wolves attacked.

Black Hawk stirred in his bed, having heard his sled dogs barking loudly. He pulled himself out of bed just as the huskies' barking changed to howling, as one of the dogs came under attack. Black Hawk could see shadows moving around aggressively in the darkness, prompting him to dress quickly. He told his wife there was an emergency with the sled dogs and they needed his help immediately. He grabbed his rifle and bolted out the cabin door.

The scene he came upon was devastating, causing Black Hawk to raise his rifle and shoot two rounds into the fray of the now psychotic wolf pack, whose only intent was killing one of his huskies. The wolves had attacked one of his sled dogs, killing it. Two wolves also lay in the blood-soaked snow, dead from bullets shot from Black Hawk's rifle. The remaining wolves had managed to escape into the bush, leaving the other huskies silent, mourning the loss of one of their brothers.

Wolf attacks such as this on sled dogs were rare but did happen occasionally. Black Hawk dragged the bodies of the dead canines behind the fur shed, placing them out of sight of his dog team, who did not want to be reminded of the incident they had just witnessed. Daylight was creeping into the early morning sky when Black Hawk finished removing the bodies. He reassured each sled dog with a loving hug, trying to show how he cared for them. He then returned to the cabin, to a waiting wife who was up and boiling water on the woodstove for coffee.

Black Hawk explained the circumstances, which had led to the death of one of their dogs and the killing of the two wolves, to his wife. Like the wolverine, White Dove hated wolves, wanting their bodies taken to a desolate place where scavengers would consume them. White Dove thought this would be a fitting end for these evil wolves.

Black Hawk let Nicky, who was whining at the front door, outside. She was curious as to what all the commotion outside earlier had been about. Finding the dead bodies of her fellow canines was not a pleasant surprise. Nicky had witnessed one other incident between dogs and wolves, which also ended in tragedy for both species. Nicky was glad she had avoided this situation; thankful she had been at the right place at the right time.

CHAPTER FOURTEEN

Sitting at their table discussing what they should do with the bodies of the wolves, the couple decided to take the dead animals to Steward's cabin. Steward had a passion for skinning wolves and preparing their hides to be used as ceremonial pieces. During special celebrations, the Indigenous people used the hides for decorative purposes and costumes for dancing. The wolf was cast as an evil entity by this community but was still viewed as sacred and a respected member of nature.

Black Hawk prepared the dogsled and loaded the dead wolves on to it. He moved the dead husky into the fur shed, locking the door to protect it from scavengers. The couple would think about how they would dispose of the sled dog when Black Hawk returned from Steward and Blossom's cabin. Nicky would stay home with White Dove, while Black Hawk took the dead wolves to Steward's cabin. He planned to drop the bodies off and, after a brief visit, make the return trip home. If all went as expected, he would only be gone for three hours.

A brief time later, Black Hawk left with his unusually quiet dog team, which was now missing one of its members.

Only the sound of the runners sliding over the snow broke the silence of the Yukon morning. Being down one dog, meant the other huskies had to pull harder to keep up with their pace. Black Hawk would try to purchase a husky while in Dawson at Christmastime with money the couple had saved for such an emergency.

After an uneventful journey, Black Hawk and his team arrived at Steward's cabin with the frozen wolves tied on the sled. Steward was thrilled to have what he considered a bounty. Wolves were hard to find and shoot in the bush. This forest, which the wolves had called home for thousands of years, was their safety net. It provided the animals with thick cover, which allowed them to avoid their greatest enemy, humans with guns.

Black Hawk wished Steward and Blossom goodbye, glad to be rid of the carcasses he had carried on the dogsled. The huskies were happier not having to smell the strong scent of the dead wolves on their return trip. The dogs pulled exuberantly on their journey back home, knowing they would be fed when they completed their journey.

Black Hawk arrived home in the early of the afternoon. He realized he needed fish to feed his hungry dogs. Entering the warm cabin, he told his wife the trip was successful, and Steward and Blossom had sent their best wishes to her. Black Hawk also asked White Dove if she wanted to join him in a fishing excursion, as they needed more fish to feed the dogs.

The couple added wood to the stove and left Nicky in the cabin. Black Hawk mushed his dogs onto the frozen surface of the lake, with White Dove riding in the sled. Within a brief time, they were at the holes in the ice used for fishing. Black Hawk broke through the new ice which had formed since their last visit. The couple spent the next hour pulling whitefish and lake trout out of the hole, feeding the fresh fish to the hungry dogs. This feast on the lake took the dogs' minds off the horrific events they had witnessed this morning at their kennel, the death of one of their own by the pack of hungry wolves.

CHAPTER FIFTEEN

After a successful fishing trip, the couple returned to the cabin with the sled dogs. The animals' stomachs were full, and the dogs portrayed a cheerful disposition when Black Hawk returned them to their kennel. The fish the couple brought home went into the outdoor freezer, with Black Hawk keeping out one large lake trout for dinner and a whitefish to feed Nicky later. After finishing his outside chores, Black Hawk returned to the comfort of the cabin, where White Dove had stoked the fire in the belly of the woodstove and added fuel. Grey smoke flowed from the chimney, as the smouldering embers lay in the bottom of the stove. The new wood lying on top finally caught fire, sending a radiating warmth throughout the couple's cabin.

After warming up for thirty minutes, Black Hawk walked out to the fur shed to clean the lake trout for dinner. His frozen sled dog lay dead in the corner of the room. He knew he had to produce a plan as to what to do with this body. At times, early fur trappers were forced to make decisions they did not like to undertake. Black Hawk decided to sacrifice his dog, using his body as bait to draw in the hungry wolf pack. These predators would like the idea of eating their arch enemy, the husky. He finished cleaning the trout, taking the filets and inners back to the cabin. Nicky would be fed the remains of the trout outside the cabin, along with her whitefish, while the couple ate their dinner inside. Black Hawk and White Dove discussed their trapline, planning to awaken tomorrow at sunrise to check their traps for fur.

Black Hawk told White Dove about his plan to use the dead sled dog to lure the wolf pack to what they would think was a free dinner. Black Hawk was worried the hungry wolves would return to his cabin and kill another one of his dogs, surmising if he could kill two more wolves in the pack, the rest of the animals would no longer feel safe and move to a different area. Hopefully, the wolves would move miles away from the hand of man and his gun, which were slowly eliminating this wolf family. White Dove agreed with Black Hawk's plan. The dog would be left in the fur shed until the couple were ready to seek their revenge against the wolf pack.

The Yukon night was gorgeous, with a cloudless sky filled with shining stars and a full moon sending light into the dark forest. White Dove retrieved a deer hide her mother had given her. She and Black Hawk bundled up and went outside to sit on the hide to enjoy a peaceful evening together under this perfect umbrella of love, the night sky. Black Hawk lit a campfire to keep the couple warm. They watched the sky and wished upon a falling star.

The wood in the campfire crackled, sending the flames and smoke skyward. Occasionally the sound of a wayward owl living in the trees could be heard, its baritone hoot echoing through the silent forest. As the couple let the campfire burn down to embers, they fell asleep in each other's arms. White Dove woke Black Hawk and the couple returned to their home to go to bed. The cabin in the woods shone like one of the stars above it, an oasis of peace in a sometimes gentle land.

CHAPTER SIXTEEN

The dogs were pulling at their harnesses, ready to leave the cabin and get to work. The dogs were taking Black Hawk and White Dove to check the traps they had set two days earlier. Black Hawk was up with the sun, preparing the sled dogs for their perceived adventure today. He mushed the animals to the cabin, where he picked up his wife. Once White Dove settled in, the dogs knew they had picked up their last rider and shot forward before Black Hawk gave the command to go. Black Hawk let the dogs run, the trail was good, and the animals needed to burn off some of the nervous energy which gripped them.

Black Hawk slowed the dogs to their first stop. As he walked over to his set, he was shocked and dismayed to find a half-eaten weasel, all that remained of this once nice fur. A wolverine had discovered their trapline on the first day, reminding Black Hawk why this animal was a fur trapper's worst enemy. He reset the trap, using fish as bait. Returning to the sled, he told White Dove the unwelcome news, stressing how important it was to kill the wolverine. This predator could cause enough damage to severely limit the amount of money they could earn for the season.

The couple moved on down the line, not seeing any activity around their traps until they reached the fourth one. There, a larger animal lay dead in the snow. Excitement mounted in Black Hawk's chest, curious as to what they had caught. Another surprise awaited this lucky trapper; it was the wolverine, who mistakenly thought another easy meal was here for the taking. Unfortunately for this hapless animal, he got his head caught in the steel trap, killing him instantly while trying to eat the bait.

White Dove's eyes shone as brightly as the full moon when she saw Black Hawk carrying the dead wolverine back to the sled. Nature had taken care of this problem animal for them. The rest of the trapline produced two pine martens and an ermine, a weasel who wears a coat of white instead of brown during the winter. Black Hawk guided his dogs onto the beaver pond, to check the one trap he had set there.

The swamp was quiet, except for the call of a lonely raven looking for a friend. The beaver trap was empty, as these smart animals were not easy to catch. As Black Hawk turned his sled around to head home, he noted the menacing looking storm clouds moving into the area, signalling the approach of another storm.

On their way to the cabin, Black Hawk mushed the dogs toward the evergreen thicket where the rabbit snares had been set. Black Hawk retrieved three rabbits and found evidence of another rabbit having been snared and eaten by a raptor. The large bird had left only the animal's fur and blood lying in the white snow.

Black Hawk pointed the sled dogs in the direction of home, a light snow starting to fall as the couple arrived back at their cabin. The peace of mind of being home was a feeling of comfort and safety in this often unforgiving land.

CHAPTER SEVENTEEN

The snow fell harder, signaling more severe weather to come. Black Hawk put the dogs in their respective places. Before joining White Dove in the cabin, he went to the freezer to retrieve moose meat, while White Dove carried extra firewood in from the outside pile, placing it beside the woodstove. The wind began to blow hard, rattling the cabin windows which were not tightly sealed.

Black Hawk told White Dove as soon as the warm weather returned, they would make the cabin more airtight. Because of cracks in the logs, cold drafts were entering the cabin, making it difficult to heat. This caused the couple to burn extra firewood, which was a valuable commodity not be wasted. Nicky snored loudly, asleep by the woodstove, oblivious to the storm raging outside.

The blizzard blew hard all night, blowing the snow against the cabin. By early morning, the storm had moved through the area, leaving clearing skies. Black Hawk and White Dove lay in bed, the fire in the woodstove and their blankets keeping them warm. Today they would dig out their traps which were now buried under the new snow. Black Hawk reluctantly got up and let a whining Nicky out the front door of the cabin. He then returned to his wife, joining her in bed. A sense of calm swept over the couple as the quiet engulfed them, capturing their spirits and leaving them with a feeling of thankfulness.

A barking Nicky alerted Black Hawk to look outside. Nicky had a red fox cornered against the cabin wall. Without hesitation, Black Hawk grabbed his rifle, opened the front door, and shot the unsuspecting fox at close range. The bullet hit the animal in the head, killing him instantly. The fox would make a nice fur to add to the others, which were frozen and waiting to be processed in the fur shed.

Black Hawk dressed, leaving the cabin to prepare the dogsled to check his traps. The couple would skip breakfast, waiting to eat when they returned home. A foot of new snow covered the ground. The dogs pulled hard on their harnesses, breaking the trail, and pulling the sled through the deep, fluffy snow. The couple rescued the buried traps from under the new snow. Two of the traps held pine martens, a small mammal plentiful in the northern forest, and a surprise awaited the couple when they checked their last trap on their trapline. The couple had trapped their first beaver, a full-grown adult male. The couple rejoiced at their luck, as Black Hawk pulled the catch out of the hole in the ice. The beaver pelt was valuable, and its meat was a favorite among early trappers living in the bush.

Black Hawk loaded the heavy animal onto the sled, reset the beaver trap, turned his dog team around, and mushed the animals home. He left the rabbit snares buried in the snow, knowing they would be impossible to find. Waiting to set new snares until the rabbits made new runways in the deep snow made the most sense to Black Hawk. The couple would soon be home, where the arduous work would begin, processing all the fur sitting in the shed. It was a task neither Black Hawk nor White Dove were looking forward to.

CHAPTER EIGHTEEN

Black Hawk left the cabin and walked to the fur shed. He wanted to start a fire in the woodstove, allowing the building to warm enough to thaw the frozen mammals whose hides needed to be removed. He then returned to the cabin, where he and his wife had decided to take a nap. Their visit to the trapline left them cold and tired, making getting warm under the blankets a priority. They would plan to work late to finish preparing the fur they had trapped.

The couple's nap was interrupted by Nicky barking, indicating she wanted outside. Black Hawk pulled himself out of bed, granting the dog's wish. He woke White Dove, telling her he was going to the fur shed to stoke the fire and check the animal pelts, to see if they were thawing. Once there, he moved the carcass of his frozen sled dog to a secure place outside the heated shed, as he did not want the body to thaw while the couple were processing the other mammals. Before returning to the cabin, he fed his sled dogs dinner, one white fish for each of them from the outdoor freezer.

By the time Black Hawk and Nicky returned to the cabin, White Dove was out of bed frying moose meat on the woodstove. Black Hawk told his wife after they finished eating, the animals in the shed would be ready for processing. Nicky could wait to eat, as she would be fed the remains from the animals they would be working on.

The evening sky was darkening, when the couple, with Nicky in tow, walked to the fur shed. Under lamp light and the light from the moon, they would use the long worktable in the shed, which could accommodate both while working. The young fur trappers were experienced preparing furs, as they had both previously collaborated with their fathers, who had taught their children how to harvest the fur of mammals living in the forest.

Black Hawk and White Dove got to work, deciding to skin the pine martens and ermine first, the smallest animals they had caught in their steel traps. The red fox Nicky had cornered at the cabin and the wolverine they caught on the trapline were the next furs to be worked on. This left the beaver, which Black Hawk said he would butcher himself. He told White Dove he would be careful not to damage the valuable hide when he processed the animal for its meat.

Finishing his work in the shed, Black Hawk carried some beaver meat to the cabin for White Dove to cook. The rest of the meat he placed in the outdoor freezer, to be eaten this winter. The remains of the animals they had processed would be used as bait for their traps and food for their huskies.

The Yukon night was quiet, causing drowsiness to take over the tired couple. They retired to bed early, wanting to be rested to start this process all over again in the morning. The life of a fur trapper can become monotonous, repeating the same jobs daily. However, the majority of these hardened men and women would have it no other way.

CHAPTER NINETEEN

Upon awakening the next morning, Black Hawk dressed quickly. While in bed the night before, he had told White Dove he was going to check the trapline early, by himself. Upon his return, they would hatch a plan for luring the wolves into a deadly trap, using their dead sled dog as bait. Before checking on his dog team, Black Hawk placed the dead husky in the fur shed and lit a fire in the stove, to allow the body to begin thawing.

Once outside, the dogs were frisky and ready to go for a run. Black Hawk harnessed the huskies to the sled, then left to check the trapline. He planned to also set rabbit snares before returning home. The dogs ran fast and pulled hard, glad to be free of the restraints which confined them at home. The first trap yielded a bobcat, which Black Hawk had to shoot. Its leg was caught in the trap and the animal was angry and in pain. One bullet to the head put the bobcat out of its misery. A weasel and a pine marten finished out the day's total of fur caught. Black Hawk mushed his dog team home, happy with what his traps yielded today.

Black Hawk dropped off the day's catch at the outdoor freezer, not wanting the animals to thaw out in the warming fur shed. He placed his dogs back into their kennels and returned to the cabin, where White Dove was waiting for him. He told his wife about the bobcat with its leg caught in the trap and how he had to shoot the animal. She shook her head at the bobcat's misfortune. Black Hawk also told her he had thought about a way to deal with the wolves. While out running the line today, he had been watching for an ideal spot to set a trap for them. One area he passed through, always seemed to have fresh wolf tracks, which could indicate their den was close. Black Hawk thought this area would be the perfect spot to put out his bait and wait for the hungry wolves to come. He said there was a place which offered good cover and should provide for an excellent shot at these predators he would like to see gone from their property forever.

White Dove thought the plan sounded perfect and in the afternoon the couple left the cabin with the thawed body of the dead sled dog. After reaching the area Black Hawk had described, they unloaded their morbid cargo and set the trap. White Dove returned to the cabin with the dog team, to prevent the wolves from catching their scent. Black Hawk sought cover and waited to see if the wolves would respond as he hoped.

The smell of a dead animal has a distinctive odour to a wolf, which Black Hawk believed would make the wolves come investigate where the smell was coming from when they left their den before sunset. With luck, the animals would come here first, before dark. He and White Dove had agreed she would return for him thirty minutes after sunset, as once the night settled in Black Hawk would no longer be able to see his prey well enough to get a clear shot at them with his rifle.

Black Hawk managed to get into a comfortable position as he waited for the wolves to make an appearance. Two hours went by with no movement. The sky was darkening, as the first signs of dusk made its appearance. Black Hawk listened to short howls coming from the forest. Shortly after dusk, the wolves showed their faces, emerging from the forest and approaching the dead husky. A primal instinct gripped the canines as they savagely attacked the dead dog, making dinner out of him. The wolves' inattention gave Black Hawk time to fire off three shots. While a few wolves managed to retreat into the bush, in the fading light Black Hawk saw two new bodies lying in the snow.

Black Hawk came out of hiding to examine the corpses. Two wolves lay dead in the snow, while a mortally wounded third animal had left a blood trail leaving the area. Black Hawk knew this animal would die from blood loss, the bright arterial blood visible in the white snow. He decided to drag all the bodies, including the sled dog, into the bush and let nature take its course. White Dove would rather hear about what happened than see it. With certainty she would not want to take the bodies home, leaving him no choice but to remove them from sight, a choice his wife would be happy he made.

CHAPTER TWENTY

Black Hawk had just finished disposing of the bodies of the wolves and sled dog in the forest when he heard his dogs barking. It was White Dove, approaching with the team to pick him up. She was pleasantly surprised to hear of the events which took place while she was gone, happy Black Hawk had killed two, maybe three, wolves who belonged to the pack which were responsible for killing one of their dogs. The pack would soon be down to three wolves, with those left leaving the area, looking for a safer place to live.

The couple returned to their cabin, pleased with the results of their mission to kill the marauding wolves. These predators had often made nighttime appearances at their cabin, antagonizing their sled dogs. Black Hawk hoped this problem had been taken care of, with the deaths of three more wolves from the pack. He returned the dogs to their yard and fed them the last of the whitefish from the outdoor freezer.

Returning to the cabin, Black Hawk found his wife frying venison on the woodstove for dinner. The month of December was passing quickly, the couple kept busy working their trapline and harvesting the fur they caught in their traps. The Christmas season would soon be upon them, which meant their trip to Dawson was just over a week away. Both Black Hawk and White Dove were looking forward to seeing everyone again, especially for the holiday.

Wendy and Jason had invited the couple to join in the family celebration, including dinner and a celebratory Christmas tree for everyone to enjoy. The trappers who made up this group of family and friends in the bush, gathered at Wendy and Jason's home for Christmas every year. The prerequisite for joining the celebration was bringing a gift for the person whose name they had picked at the moose hunt, as well as some frozen meat, if they possessed enough to share. The offering of food would go to feed the hungry in Dawson. Black Hawk would take moose meat, as the amount of venison in their freezer was getting low.

The couple ate their dinner in silence, listening to the whistling wind which howled around the cabin, rattling the glass in the cabin windows. After eating, the couple relaxed by playing a game of cards. They enjoyed playing poker, using glass beads as a substitute for money. After a late night, the couple counted their beads, proclaiming White Dove the winner. Black Hawk and White Dove put the cards away and retired to bed. They lay awake listening to the sounds coming from the forest which surrounded their lonely cabin. It was an oasis of peace in a land fraught with danger, a land in Canada's north.

CHAPTER TWENTY-ONE

The couple slept comfortably in their warm bed, the burning wood in the stove radiating its heat throughout the cozy cabin. The north wind blew hard, blowing the snow in a whirlwind around the log structure Black Hawk and White Dove called home.

The morning sun shone through the frost-covered glass of the cabin window. Black Hawk opened his eyes, listening to the silence which surrounded him. The sudden sound of a raven's call pierced the quiet northern air. Black Hawk lay still with his eyes open. His thoughts took him to his past, when he was a young boy growing up with his parents in a small Indigenous village in the Yukon wilderness. Realizing he was no longer that boy, he wrapped his arms around his wife, who lay beside him.

The day was sunny, but cold. Black Hawk planned to wake White Dove soon, wanting to take his dog team and go fishing on the lake to catch whitefish for them to eat. He pulled himself out of bed, letting a whining Nicky outside to use the bathroom. White Dove was awake when he returned to bed. She snuggled against Black Hawk, hugging him tightly, not wanting to let him go. Nicky's barking to be let into the cabin brought the young couple back to reality.

Both Black Hawk and White Dove got out of bed, now ready to start their day. White Dove placed the kettle of water on the cooktop of the woodstove to boil. Black Hawk had stoked the embers of the remaining coals and added wood to the fire when he was up earlier to let Nicky out. After finishing his coffee, Black Hawk went outside to harness the dogs, who were hungry and ready to eat. Black Hawk thought of how difficult it was trying to find enough food to keep the work dogs fed. This morning, the huskies would have to wait for their breakfast.

Black Hawk mushed the dogs onto the lake, an open expanse of snow lay before them. With added enthusiasm, the sled dogs pulled hard on their harnesses, knowing where they were going. Ten minutes later, Black Hawk slowed his dogs, as they neared the holes in the ice used for fishing. The sled dogs were excited, knowing they would soon be fed.

Black Hawk took the axe he had brought with him and reopened the holes in the ice, allowing White Dove to get her fishing net into the water. Within a brief time, whitefish littered the ice around the open holes the fish had been pulled from. A good fishing day meant extra food for the huskies, a treat the dogs did not often enjoy, as being constantly hungry was the norm for these working canines.

Satisfied with their catch, the couple packed up the fish and their gear and headed home. The sled dogs, now energized from eating, wanted to run. Black Hawk obliged his dog team, giving Chief, his lead dog, the opportunity to manage his subordinates, free of micromanaging him. The dogs, led by the alpha male, raced across the open snow until they reached the opposite side of the lake. Upon reaching this point, they turned suddenly, following the shoreline at a steady trot.

White Dove nudged Black Hawk, pointing to an abandoned cabin set back in a wooded area of the forest, now visible, as the trees were bare of leaves. Black Hawk steered his dog team towards the structure. This was the cabin which now belonged to Gerald, the man they had met previously, who had shared his crazy plans, which neither Black Hawk nor White Dove believed would ever come to fruition. Once onshore, the only signs of life around the cabin were the tracks of a fox, who was using the cover of the old logs for its home. During the winter, even the animals need to take shelter from the elements.

CHAPTER TWENTY-TWO

Finding nothing more of interest, Black Hawk turned the dogs around and left the area, heading in the direction of home. The sled dogs, knowing where they were going, ran at a fast trot back to the cabin. Upon arrival, Black Hawk unloaded the fish into the freezer, except for one lake trout which he would clean for White Dove to cook for dinner. He returned the dogs to their kennel and joined White Dove in the cabin for coffee.

The couple discussed their trip to Dawson, which would be happening soon. They planned to pull all their traps from the bush and place them in the fur shed. They would resume trapping when they returned from their trip to Wendy and Jason's house in Dawson. At that time, they were going to increase the number of traps on their trapline to fifteen, from the ten they currently had set.

The couple decided to make room to take a bundle of hides with them on the sled to sell in Dawson. The hides from their early season haul were in high demand, with record prices being paid by brokers who could not satisfy the demand for fur which was sweeping across Europe. The couple had collected the mammals they caught daily, keeping them together in the fur shed. Before leaving for Dawson, they would prepare the hides to take with them. Black Hawk and White Dove would use the money from the furs they sold to buy needed supplies for themselves and their dogs, and perhaps an additional dog for their team.

Tomorrow Black Hawk would check the trapline for the last time before departing for their Christmas adventure to Dawson. He planned to collect the traps until they returned home. The accumulation of frozen mammals in the fur shed would be thawed and processed, the skins taken with them to sell in Dawson.

The following morning came early; an overcast sky greeting the couple as they left the cabin. Black Hawk had risen with the daylight, the sunrise unseen through the thick cloud cover. The couple checked their trapline, gathering a small catch of mammals in the traps. They retrieved the steel traps, carrying them back to the cabin, along with the day's catch. The trip back to their cabin was uneventful.

When they returned, Black Hawk unloaded the dogsled, putting the traps and the animals they had caught in the fur shed. When Black Hawk was finished, he lit a fire in the woodstove, needing the frozen mammals to thaw before their hides could be taken from them. After dinner, the couple would start this work, not finishing until after midnight. Tomorrow would be a day of rest, followed by one more day at home preparing for their trip to Wendy and Jason's house, a Christmas celebration the couple were looking forward to.

CHAPTER TWENTY-THREE

White Dove cooked the lake trout Black Hawk had cleaned for dinner. The smell of fish frying on the stove filled the cabin with an aroma which tantalized the taste buds of both man and dog, the latter who was waiting patiently to eat. Black Hawk and White Dove ate first, with Nicky, the family pet, receiving only bites of food broken off the filets the couple were eating for dinner. Black Hawk planned on feeding Nicky her fill from the remains of the mammals which were waiting to be processed for their fur.

After eating, Black Hawk and White Dove prepared themselves for a long evening in the fur shed. They had a variety of animals to process, each wearing a valuable coat of fur. The couple walked to their work site, where they sorted the now thawing animals into piles. Pine martens made up the largest group, as they were the most abundant animal in the area. Two beavers, their fur unprocessed, were the most valuable pelts in the couple's fur shed. A lynx and two red foxes were included in this hodge podge of animals Black Hawk had caught on the trapline.

The couple got to work, removing the hides of the animals which lay in piles on the floor beside them. After working diligently for hours processing the fur, the couple finally finished. The beavers were butchered for their meat, which was added to the winter supply of food in the outdoor freezer. Nicky had a full stomach from overeating and wanted to go back to the cabin where she would sleep by the woodstove. Black Hawk obliged the dog's wishes, letting her into the cabin and closing the door behind her.

The couple sorted the remains of the other animals, keeping most for bait for their traps. The unusable portions of the slaughtered animals would be dumped in the forest in the morning, the body parts left for scavengers to eat. With that last thought in mind, Black Hawk and White Dove locked up the fur shed and returned to their cabin. Upon entering their home, a blast of warm air warmed their faces, the heat radiating from the hot belly of the woodstove. Nicky lay asleep, snoring and dreaming about her canine boyfriends. Dreams of romance, but never finding true love, were always the disappointing factors for Nicky during these dreams.

Black Hawk and White Dove undressed and climbed into bed. They pulled the warm covers over them and snuggled into each other's arms. The silence in the forest surrounding them helped send the couple into an undisturbed sleep for the night. The cabin had great potential, sitting in a no man's land of forests and wilderness lakes. The structure was an anomaly in the forest, a beacon of love and hope for Black Hawk and White Dove, the couple who lived in this land which time forgot.

CHAPTER TWENTY-FOUR

The morning sun shone brilliantly through the cabin windows. The sound of a woodpecker's beak hitting the hollow tree where the bird lived was the only sound to break the quiet of the forest which surrounded them. Black Hawk pulled himself out of bed to perform his morning rituals, letting Nicky outside, stoking the fire and adding more wood, and putting the kettle on the woodstove to boil. These were chores Black Hawk performed every morning before starting his day, which also included returning to the bed with his wife for a brief time while waiting for the water to get hot.

After breakfast, Black Hawk suggested to his wife they go fishing today. The couple needed food for their dogs to eat while on their trip, and during their stay in Dawson. With money from the sale of their furs, Black Hawk planned to buy dried dog food to supplement the fish diet his sled dogs lived almost exclusively on. Black Hawk prepared the dog team for a trip onto the lake, another repetitious job which had to be performed regularly to provide enough protein to keep his dogs healthy.

After being on the ice for two hours, the couple had a

large catch of fish. Black Hawk noticed a subtle change in the weather, as the once clear sky was full of dark clouds. The wind had shifted, now blowing from the north, Black Hawk and White Dove feeling the bitter cold on their faces. The couple picked up their fish off the ice and loaded the sled for their return trip to their cabin. The dogs, sensing a storm was coming, ran home with abandon, pulling hard on their harnesses.

Once home, Black Hawk handed White Dove a large trout from the dogsled, telling her to take the fish into the cabin. He then stored the rest of the bounty of food on the worktable in the unheated fur shed. He returned the dogs to their yard, buttoning down the hatches for the expected snowstorm. Snow flurries were blowing against his face as he finished with his dogs and walked toward the cabin.

Entering the home, Black Hawk found White Dove cooking a piece of moose meat she had taken out of the freezer this morning to thaw. The rich aroma of the wild meat cooking made him realize how hungry he was. The storm hit with a fury, shaking the cabin, and testing its strength against the wrath of Mother Nature. The blizzard blew all night, ending like others, by sunrise the following morning.

The dissipating snowstorm moved away, to threaten someone else's day. Peering outside, the onlookers marveled in silence as to the power which befell the planet overnight; a cleansing which left a cloak of white over the landscape, which could never be duplicated by man. This was a land where the powers of the unknown made the decisions and controlled the destiny of those who lived here, where man had few choices in the place he shared with nature.

CHAPTER TWENTY-FIVE

Black Hawk and White Dove spent the day preparing for their trip to Dawson. They had been invited to a Christmas celebration held at Wendy and Jason's house. All the couples, their children, and family dogs who lived in the forest, trapping fur, were invited to attend. It would include a social gathering around the Christmas tree, healthy food, and lively conversations. Black Hawk and White Dove planned to leave their cabin early tomorrow morning, so they spent most of the day organizing the few personal belongings they would be taking with them.

Black Hawk and White Dove ate an early dinner, lake trout being on the menu. After eating the delicious fish, the couple played cards for two hours before deciding to go to bed. By lamplight, they read books which they had started but never finished, as the anticipation about leaving tomorrow made it hard for them to fall asleep. Soon the tranquility which surrounded the cabin sent the young couple into a sound slumber until the following morning.

Black Hawk stirred in bed, rolling over and opening his eyes. White Dove lay beside him; he reached over and pulled her close to him. Black Hawk could not imagine how lonely he would be living here without his wife. He finally pulled himself out of bed and walked to the window of the cabin, looking outside. A bright sun, just rising above the horizon, greeted Black Hawk. This meant a probable sunny day for travelling. He woke White Dove and let Nicky, who was waiting at the cabin door, outside. The couple dressed, and Black Hawk went outside to prepare the dog team and load the fur on the sled.

The dogs would be forced to move at a slower pace than usual on the trip to Wendy and Jason's house. One adult and Nicky would have to run beside the sled until they reached their destination, to accommodate the furs they were taking to town. Black Hawk and White Dove would take turns between running and riding, with Nicky able to sit on the rider's lap to rest on occasion.

Black Hawk readied the sled and mushed his dog team to the cabin to pick up a waiting White Dove. He secured the cabin door and placed the bag of their personal belongings on the sled. The entourage left the cabin, the small structure soon disappearing. The day was sunny, and the winds were calm as the dogs pulled the sled towards Dawson.

With the sun directly overhead, Black Hawk and White Dove decided to stop for lunch. The group had reached the lake, which was the halfway point to Dawson. The dogs needed a rest and were each fed a whitefish for lunch. The couple looked over the expanse of the frozen lake, a desolate but beautiful scene. It provided a wilderness picture, snapped by the eyes of the couple, which would become a memory that would last forever.

CHAPTER TWENTY-SIX

After a thirty-minute rest at the lake, Black Hawk and White Dove left the area to continue their journey to Dawson. The afternoon passed quickly, with the dogs enthusiastically pulling, hoping their journey would soon be over. Twilight was approaching as the smoke from the chimneys of the homes in Dawson came into view. The gray smoke from the woodfires left an odour in the air which enshrouded the town in a thick smog. Luckily, Wendy and Jason lived far enough outside of Dawson City they never experienced the haze which seemed trapped there.

As the couple drew closer to town, the trail they were on intersected with another trail from the north. Black Hawk was surprised to see Grey Wolf and Rose heading straight toward them. They were also on their way to Jason and Wendy's for Christmas. The two couples stopped briefly, laughing about running into each other again on the trail. After exchanging greetings and hugs, they followed one another the remainder of the way.

Grey Wolf and Black Hawk mushed their dogsleds into Jason and Wendy's yard, the couples' long journeys to Dawson a success. Steward was the first to walk out of the house to greet the arriving couples. Steward was Wendy's brother, who with his wife Blossom, had arrived in Dawson earlier to help Wendy and Jason prepare for the arrival of all the guests. Joe and Mary, who had been the first to arrive, also came out of the house, accompanied by Wendy and Jason, to greet their arriving company. Like Black Hawk and White Dove, Joe and Mary were not blood relatives, but had been accepted into this close-knit group and treated as family members.

The men moved their dogsleds to a location near the barn, with Black Hawk removing the bundle of furs from his sled and storing them inside the structure. The area where the men kept their dogs had been prepared years ago, when Bev, the previous owner of the home had hosted Christmas parties for her family, which included her siblings who lived near Dawson at the time. All her brothers and sisters were just a memory now, passed away, joining their ancestors in the afterlife.

The mood was joyous when the men returned to the house. Wendy had a moose stew cooking on the woodstove, made with vegetables from her root cellar. The smell of hot bread baking in the oven filled the house with an aroma even the dogs loved. Black Hawk and White Dove had arrived just in time for dinner. They sat down in the kitchen and enjoyed a large bowl of stew with fresh baked bread. Eating well and enjoying good company were the prerequisites for this party.

After a delicious supper, the group of friends and family retired to the living room to enjoy the Christmas tree. Wendy and Jason let their son, Kuzih, and their nephew,

Grey Eagle, hang the decorations their company had created and brought with them, a tradition Bev had started years ago. The Christmas tree in the corner of the room shone like a beacon of hope to the people who lived in this unforgiving land. A place which offered a hard life to all who lived here.

The evening passed quickly, with Wendy and Shining Star taking their sons upstairs to bed early. The rest of the party stayed up late, enjoying the opportunity to talk to other people who shared similar interests. Trapping stories were exchanged and real-life adventures with wildlife were discussed. The full moon and shining stars, their light reflecting off the white snow, lit up the beautiful landscape with natural light, putting on a display of nature for the lucky souls living in this land called the Yukon.

CHAPTER TWENTY-SEVEN

Black Hawk lay in bed, having awakened fifteen minutes earlier; he was listening to Wendy making noise in the kitchen. Like her predecessor, Wendy was the first one in the kitchen, preparing for a breakfast crowd. Once this task was accomplished, she would then begin working on the Christmas Eve dinner.

The smell of bread baking in the oven was a promising sign of the delicious breakfast the fur trappers would be given. Fresh eggs gathered from the chickens in the barn and pork Wendy had purchased in town would round out the breakfast menu. Black Hawk thought about his day, wanting to visit the fur broker in Dawson to sell his furs. The couple would use the money to buy needed supplies for their dogs and themselves. He would also inquire about any sled dogs for sale, looking to replace their dog who had been killed.

Black Hawk left White Dove sleeping, heading downstairs, following the aroma of fresh coffee coming from the kitchen. Blossom was busy in the kitchen, helping Wendy keep a sense of order. The hungry visitors, who were beginning to invade the kitchen, were sent to the living room, and told they would be notified when breakfast was ready. Wendy told the group the only reason she wanted to see anyone in the kitchen was for a cup of coffee. Black Hawk walked back upstairs to wake White Dove. Opening the door, he was surprised to see her up and dressed, ready to go downstairs for breakfast. She told Black Hawk she was awakened by all the loud activity downstairs.

The couple joined the rest of the group in the living room, waiting to be called to breakfast by the cooks in the kitchen. Wendy and Blossom set up a buffet-style arrangement for the food, letting the visitors select what they wanted. This was a one of a kind, first buffet style breakfast served in the Dawson area, something which not even the hotels were featuring.

The food was delicious and plentiful, the diners thankful for the meal. After breakfast, the women cleaned up the mess left by the breakfast crowd, including washing all the dishes. The men went to check their sled dogs and feed the hungry animals. Wendy asked Black Hawk and White Dove if they would also feed the donkeys in the barn. After feeding their sled dogs, the couple entered the barn, calling out to Omar and Honey by name. The animals' reactions were a multitude of welcoming sounds from the four donkeys living in the barn. The donkeys were very loving, rubbing their necks against the bodies of Black Hawk and White Dove as the couple patted the happy animals' heads.

When Black Hawk and White Dove finished feeding and watering the donkeys, they left the barn and returned to the house. Black Hawk told Wendy he was taking furs they had brought from home to sell in Dawson. After the sale was completed, the couple would run errands and then return to get ready for dinner and other festivities planned for this evening. Jason was planning a special tribute to their late benefactor, Wendy's Aunt Bev. Although Black Hawk and White Dove had never met her, they knew they had been gifted their home because of her kindness.

Bev had dedicated her life to giving to the community, many of whom had to do without the things Bev had been blessed with. Jason had a surprise, which no one in this group would ever guess. Earlier in the year, he had secured two cases of fine wine in Dawson and stored them just for this occasion. The tribute to Bev would begin with a toast, followed by a short speech from Wendy praising her aunt's kind spirit. Bev was an icon in Dawson, who would never be forgotten by her family or friends.

Black Hawk prepared the dog team, loading the furs on the sled. Nicky would stay home to enjoy the company of her canine friends, who had come with their owners to Wendy and Jason's. White Dove joined her husband, holding the bale of fur on her lap. She would ride this way to the fur broker's business in town. With a yell from Black Hawk, the dog team pulled the sled and occupants toward Dawson.

CHAPTER TWENTY-EIGHT

After a brief ride, Black Hawk and White Dove arrived at their destination. The broker was a pleasant man, with a calming demeanour and a contagious laugh. He examined the hides the couple brought him, checking each one carefully for flaws or damage to the fur. He told the couple they had done an excellent job of harvesting the fur and he would pay a premium for their product.

A highly valued commodity in England and other European countries, fur was in such high demand all the orders could not be filled. This kept the price of fur at its highest prices ever. Black Hawk and White Dove left the broker's office with huge smiles on their faces. They were thrilled with their good fortune at having sold their furs when the prices were high, walking out of the man's office richer than they had anticipated.

Next, the couple stopped at the livery stable to purchase dry dog food the proprietor made on the premises. Dogs in town had taken well to it, happily eating this food until their stomachs were full. This food took the pressure off dog owners having to have fish on hand to feed their always hungry sled dogs. The man also sold a special mash he made for pack animals, which White Dove bought a bag of for the donkeys Wendy kept in her barn. While at the livery stable, the couple inquired if the owner knew of any sled dogs for sale. Unfortunately, the man reported he didn't know of anyone willing to sell a dog at this time of year.

The couple's next stop was the general store, where they purchased coffee, sugar, flour, salt, and a new beaver trap. Black Hawk was certain the beaver population at home would not be harmed by the addition of one more trap. They exchanged friendly banter with the owner, who told them about all the new businesses which had recently begun operating in Dawson. He mentioned a store which opened in the latter part of the summer, and had sold out of product twice, forcing the man to close for the winter. It was a new ironware store, which sold the most up-to-date products being manufactured in the only foundry on the west coast of the United States. Black Hawk told the man when they returned to Dawson this summer, they would plan to visit this new store.

Saying goodbye to the owner of the mercantile, Black Hawk and his wife returned to Wendy and Jason's house to rejoin the party. Upon arrival, Black Hawk dropped off White Dove at the barn with the dog food and donkey treats. The rest of the items they purchased would be stored in Wendy's house until their return trip back to their cabin. Black Hawk returned the dogs to their holding area and joined White Dove in the barn, storing the dog food in a dry space. The couple fed the excited donkeys, who had enjoyed the mash before. The couple then left the barn, joining the other company in the house.

The mood was festive as these hardy men and women who lived in primitive cabins in the bush enjoyed the comforts of a large house and an all-you-can-eat buffet, always on hand to satisfy their hunger. The afternoon wore on, and soon Christmas Eve was upon these happy souls. They were enjoying each other's company tremendously, during this celebratory time of year.

When Wendy announced dinner was ready, everyone gathered around the kitchen table. A combination of venison and moose meat, supplemented by smoked trout Steward had brought, rounded out the entrée menu. Plates of potatoes, turnips, and carrots, which had been harvested from Wendy's garden and stored in her root cellar, adorned the buffet table. After everyone was seated with their food, Wendy made an announcement.

Jason carried in a crate of wine, which created startled looks upon everyone's faces. Wendy said this was a special occasion, and Bev would be the honoured guest, even if it was only in spirit. Jason poured a glass of wine for every adult at the table. First, Wendy recited the same prayer Bev always spoke before dinner. Jason then offered a toast to this woman, whom they all missed dearly at this time of year. With this last thought in mind, the group indulged in a delicious dinner.

After a festive hour of eating, the men retired to the living room with the two children, where they would wait for their wives to join them after cleaning up the mess in the kitchen. The pet dogs of the couples remained outside, waiting patiently to eat their belated Christmas Eve dinner. The wives soon joined their husbands in the living room.

Wendy and Jason had decided to move the Christmas gift exchange from Christmas morning to Christmas Eve. The participants had each selected a name at the November moose hunt, being expected to bring one gift for their assigned person. Simple items, made from materials readily available to the makers, resulted in gifts cherished by the recipients. They would serve as a reminder of the Christmas celebration these trappers enjoyed together in this wilderness community called Dawson, a treasure in Canada's growing north.

CHAPTER TWENTY-NINE

Christmas morning brought Nicky, with a set of sleigh bells tied around her neck, into Black Hawk and White Dove's bedroom. The ringing from the bells woke the couple from a deep sleep. The smell of breakfast cooking downstairs greeted the couple's senses upon awakening. Breakfast was an important gathering for these family and friends on Christmas Day.

The mood around the breakfast table was quiet, as everyone's thoughts were flooded with memories from past Christmases sitting around this very table. Bev had made Christmas Day a time for reflection and quiet, meaningful thoughts. This was why Christmas dinner, and all the celebratory aspects of the gathering, had been enjoyed on Christmas Eve. A smaller meal would be served on Christmas Day, as the visitors who had a full day's trip home, gathered up their belongings preparing to leave. These people would have to depart at daybreak to arrive at their own homes before dark.

The family and friends spent Christmas Day enjoying each other's company. They played with the children, sang carols, helped with the chores, and played cards. Before long, it was time for Christmas dinner, where Jason had two surprises for his company. First, he had acquired a smoked goose from the Indigenous couple in Dawson who sold fish to Wendy and Jason for their dogs. Fish was something which could be purchased daily, if needed. This couple had informed Jason months ago, they could supply him with a smoked goose for Christmas dinner, for a handsome fee.

The Indigenous couple shot a few of these migratory birds right before the lakes froze up, cleaning the geese and placing them in their outdoor freezer. There, the birds stayed fresh until the cold temperatures in the Yukon froze the geese and kept them frozen. At Christmastime, the birds were removed from the freezer, thawed, and smoked for the men or women who had ordered one. Such a large, cooked bird was not usually found in Dawson at this time of year.

The group of friends and family seated themselves for dinner. They were both surprised and delighted seeing the smoked goose sitting on the buffet. At dinner, Jason announced his second surprise to his guests. Each couple would receive a bottle of wine to take home with them, as he and Wendy wanted them to each have a toast to celebrate the new year. It was a wonderful ending to a perfect Christmas, a memory the fur trappers would take with them, and which would last forever.

The early morning sun started an exodus of dogsleds and their riders from Wendy and Jason's house. After being away from home for two to three days, the fur trappers were anxious to get back to their traplines and their own beds. Wendy and Jason felt likewise, exhausted from all the catering they had done for their departing company. They happily waved goodbye to each departing family member and friend.

The day was sunny, with not a cloud in the clear blue sky. Black Hawk and White Dove mushed their dogs down the trail toward home. The couple had left Wendy and Jason's at daybreak, wanting to be sure they had time to get home before darkness set in. After an uneventful trip on a beautiful sunny day, Black Hawk and White Dove could see their cabin in the distance. A brief time later the couple were home, having found their trip to Dawson both enjoyable and an experience worth repeating next year.

CHAPTER THIRTY

Black Hawk removed the extra nails he had used to secure the cabin door before leaving for Dawson. This action was a deterrent to any wayward animal who happened to stumble upon the cabin while the owners were away overnight. White Dove and Nicky entered the unheated building, with White Dove lighting the lanterns first, as twilight was approaching. She then gathered wood from the pile stacked beside the stove, starting a fire to warm the cabin to a comfortable temperature.

Black Hawk unloaded their personal gear and the supplies they had purchased in Dawson, before returning his dogs and sled to their appropriate places. He fed the dogs fish from the outdoor freezer, before returning to the cabin to join his wife and dog, glad to be home. He put a kettle of water on the now hot woodstove to brew the coffee they had purchased in town. Wendy had given the couple enough left over goose from Christmas dinner to feed themselves and Nicky tonight.

The cabin was soon cozy and warm, a steady column of smoke drifting from the chimney into the dark forest. After eating dinner, the couple, exhausted from their long

After the Gold Rush 277

trip home, retired to bed early. Sleep came swiftly, as the solitude and exhaustion they felt sent them into a deep, peaceful sleep. Three wolves circled the cabin, the desperate animals looking for food.

Just over a week ago, Black Hawk had shot and killed all the adult members of the wolf pack, leaving the three youngest wolves to fend for themselves. These young wolves, who were lost having no leadership, were starving, unable to find food. Nicky was awake, aware of the presence of these enemies outside the cabin. A low growl came from the back of the husky's throat, a warning which woke Black Hawk from his sleep. He lay still, listening to the activity outside the cabin. Black Hawk knew it was wolves by the sounds the animals were making.

Black Hawk quietly got up from the bed and walked to the cabin window. Looking outside, he noticed the outlines of three wolves, visible in the light of the moon which illuminated the area around the cabin. Nicky lay quietly by the woodstove, not wanting to be involved in what was going to happen next. Black Hawk dressed quickly, grabbed his rifle, and approached the front door of his cabin. He quietly pulled the cabin door open; the wolves paid no attention, as they were plotting their next move. Having found nothing here, they were planning to leave the area to continue their search for food.

Suddenly, two shots rang out from Black Hawk's rifle, resulting in two wolves lying dead in the front yard. White Dove shouted out, angry at Black Hawk about being awakened this way, with no warning. She told her husband she thought they were under attack by someone with a gun. Once Black Hawk explained why he had taken such desperate measures in the middle of the night, White Dove calmed down.

The remaining wolf escaped into the dark forest, hopefully to never return to the area. Black Hawk left the dead wolves where they lay, planning to deal with the bodies in the light of day. He returned to bed with White Dove, quickly falling back asleep until the first hint of dawn blessed the morning sky.

CHAPTER THIRTY-ONE

Nicky barked loudly twice, sending the message she needed to go outside now. Black Hawk reluctantly got out of bed, fulfilling the dog's wishes. Leaving the cabin, the dog walked over to examine the corpses of the wolves lying in the blood-soaked snow. Black Hawk returned to bed, where White Dove was awake. He told her he would like to process the wolves' hides because of the value of their fur. White Dove agreed with his plan, if she was not expected to help skin the wolves, which she refused to touch. He promised to keep the hides out of sight, hoping to find an out of the way place for them in the fur shed which might be problematic as they were already tight on space in this outbuilding.

While in Dawson, Black Hawk and White Dove had talked to Steward about his friend, Tim, who owned a sawmill. If their trapping season was a financial success this winter, the couple wanted to build an addition onto their fur shed, which would necessitate purchasing lumber. They needed extra storage space, as they anticipated an increase in the number of furs they expected to catch next winter, hoping to double the number of traps on their trapline.

White Dove made Black Hawk coffee and a quick breakfast of fried beaver meat, while he went out and started a fire in the shed. As he passed by the bodies in the yard, he was already anticipating an unpleasant morning. After eating, Black Hawk told his wife he would see her at lunch, kissing her goodbye and walking out the cabin door.

Black Hawk pulled the bodies of the wolves into the now warming fur shed. He noticed the column of gray smoke escaping from the chimney of the building into the wintry morning air. While waiting for the wolf carcasses to thaw, Black Hawk sharpened his knives on the grindstone. As the wolves were shot in the middle of the night, the brief time they laid in the yard did not allow them to freeze solid. This resulted in the bodies thawing out quickly in the warm shed.

Black Hawk got to work skinning the dead wolves using his sharpened knives. No other parts of the wolves would be used, their remains would be taken deep into the forest to be disposed of. At 1 p.m., he finished removing the hides, returning to the cabin to tell White Dove he was forgoing lunch. He wanted to harness the dog team and take the wolves' remains a significant distance from the cabin before it grew later in the day.

After preparing his dog team and loading the remains of the animals onto the sled, Black Hawk mushed the dogs down the trail the couple used for their trapline. Reaching the beaver dam, he guided the dogsled onto the frozen pond the beavers called home. He mushed the sled across the pond, into territory he had not yet explored. The dogs were excited, pulling harder on their harnesses, sensing or seeing something which sparked their interest.

Shortly afterwards, Black Hawk saw the anomaly which had caught the dogs' attention; a primitive shelter lay before him. As he pulled the dogs closer, Black Hawk saw the stock of a rusted rifle sticking out of the snow. Inspecting this unusual find further, he discovered the skeleton of a man, his bones scattered about this place he once called home, a shelter he had built which failed to sustain his life.

Black Hawk left the site as he found it, except for feeling it was an appropriate place to leave the remains of the two wolves. The ravens had followed Black Hawk across the beaver pond, the scent of the raw flesh of the wolves making the birds hungry. He dumped the remains close to the area where he had found the skeleton, then turned his dog team around and headed in the direction of home.

The conditions for dogsledding were perfect, the huskies, who were glad to be out of the restraints they were forced to live with, pulled the sled with enthusiasm. The dog team made it home quickly, the thoughts of filling their hungry bellies with needed food pushing them onward. Black Hawk obliged his dogs as soon as they were home, feeding them the blended dry food he had purchased from the livery stable while in Dawson for Christmas. To Black Hawk's huskies, this food was a treat, a change from the fish they were usually fed.

After feeding his dogs, Black Hawk returned to the cabin to find Nicky sleeping by the woodstove, while White Dove was knitting. He related the story of finding the skeleton in the forest to his wife. The couple wondered how this man had found himself in the situation where he ended up dying alone. That question would never be answered, as the northern wilderness had claimed another victim in the never-ending struggle for survival in this land called the Yukon.

CHAPTER THIRTY-TWO

The last week of December passed quickly. Black Hawk had decided to forgo resetting his trapline until after the start of the new year. The couple were planning a candlelight dinner, accompanied by the bottle of fine wine Wendy and Jason had given them, for New Year's Eve. Their dinner would include fresh grouse from the forest, served with potatoes and carrots Wendy had shared with them from her root cellar. White Dove had bought baking supplies during their trip and planned to bake bread in the oven to complement this special meal.

The new year would soon be upon them, and Black Hawk had not yet gone hunting for the main course for dinner. He gathered up his dog Nicky and his rifle, donned his snowshoes, and said goodbye to White Dove, as he walked out the cabin door. A stand of evergreen trees close to the house was the furthest he had to go.

Nicky bounded through the deep snow, jumping like a rabbit trying to escape a pursuing fox. Black Hawk followed closely behind his dog, signalling Nicky to wait and not enter the thicket when she reached the treeline. Nicky followed Black Hawk's orders, waiting patiently for his next instructions. After reaching his dog, Black Hawk and Nicky entered the evergreens together. Once in the thicket, Black Hawk encouraged Nicky to go ahead of him and scare up the grouse living there. She performed her job well. Using this approach for hunting, Black Hawk soon had three plump grouse in his bag, which was slung across his shoulder.

Black Hawk and Nicky happily returned to the cabin, with Black Hawk sharing the news of their successful hunt with White Dove. White Dove placed a large pot of water on the woodstove to boil. Black Hawk would soak the birds in the water, making the removal of their feathers easier. With Nicky following him, he carried the pot of hot water to the fur shed and placed it on the work bench. He submerged the grouse into the water, waiting fifteen minutes before removing their feathers.

After a tedious hour, the repetitious task of pulling feathers was finished. Tomorrow was New Year's Eve when the birds would be served for dinner. He stored the cleaned birds in the fur shed, planning to retrieve them in the morning. The frozen birds would thaw inside their cabin in time to be prepared for dinner. White Dove planned to roast the grouse in the oven and prepare the vegetables on the cook top.

New Year's Eve day turned out to be windy and cold, with even the sled dogs having a challenging time keeping warm. Black Hawk was kept busy adding firewood to the woodstove, trying to keep the cabin warm and the stove hot enough to cook the food for dinner. He hoped a successful dinner would be had on the coldest night they had experienced thus far this winter.

CHAPTER THIRTY-THREE

The smell of grouse cooking in the oven of the woodstove sent a tantalizing aroma throughout the cabin. Black Hawk, White Dove, and Nicky had spent all day indoors, as the extreme cold which had settled over Dawson and the surrounding area made it difficult to complete chores outside. The wood crackled in the stove, the heat from the fire keeping the cabin cozy and warm. Nicky lay sleeping on the floor, enjoying the warmth coming from the stove.

White Dove prepared the vegetables, placing them on the top of the stove to boil. Black Hawk retrieved the bottle of wine and placed it in the snow outside to get cold before dinner. The sky was darkening as twilight settled over this desolate land. The winds grew stronger, blowing the white powdery snow around the building. Inside the cabin, White Dove was setting the table, as dinner was almost ready.

Black Hawk retrieved the bottle of wine from outside and uncorked it. Nicky had assumed her familiar position, begging for handouts from the occupants of the table. Black Hawk removed the hot food from the oven, placing it on the table along with the vegetables. The fresh bread, which White Dove baked earlier, was added to the mix. Black

Hawk poured the wine into two cups made of pewter; a popular material used at the time for its durability.

Suggesting a toast before eating, Black Hawk wished for continued good luck living together as a happily married couple. It was their quest together, as a unified couple, which made their new life in this wilderness cabin work. After her husband's toast, White Dove said a prayer before the couple dished out the food. They consumed all the food they had cooked, except for the food they had set aside for Nicky. The happy couple enjoyed the bottle of wine with their meal, finishing it off before dinner ended.

After enjoying dinner, the couple cleaned up the table, washed the dishes, and put everything back in its proper place. The wind howled outside, showing no let up in its intensity. The deciduous trees surrounding the cabin, bare of their leaves, swayed in the strong wind, creaking and groaning.

White Dove blew out the lanterns and darkness settled over the cabin. The smoke rising from the chimney was the only sign of life surrounding this structure sitting alone in the forest. White Dove and Black Hawk felt calm in this turbulent land, their spirits one with nature.

CHAPTER THIRTY-FOUR

The early morning sun shone through the cabin windows. The high winds had slowed during the night, to a near calm. Black Hawk pulled himself out of bed, letting Nicky, who was waiting by the cabin door, outside. He then added wood to the glowing coals left in the woodstove. Within minutes, the new wood burst into flames, sending grey smoke rising from the chimney into the clear blue sky. The arctic freeze had warmed to a bearable temperature in which to work.

Black Hawk had his traps ready to reset the trapline. He woke White Dove, telling her of his plan to only set out ten traps this morning. He told his wife to stay in bed, as it would not take long and didn't require two people. He said they would wait to place the remaining ten traps tomorrow, but they needed to go fishing this afternoon to replenish the dogs' food supply.

Retrieving the remaining fish from the outdoor freezer, Black Hawk fed the huskies. After his dogs finished eating, he hooked the animals into their harnesses, loaded his traps onto the sled, and left to reset the trapline. The dogs were ambitious, glad to be up moving around, after being sedentary during the cold spell which had settled over the Yukon. Black Hawk condensed his trapline, allowing for the extra traps they would be setting tomorrow. The task went well and four hours later he was finished and on his way home.

Arriving before lunch, White Dove placed a pot of water on the stove for coffee when she heard the dogs approaching. Black Hawk settled his dogs so he could eat lunch and enjoy a cup of hot coffee before going fishing on the lake. White Dove was frying moose meat when her husband entered the cabin, the odor reminding Black Hawk how hungry he was. After lunch, the couple prepared for their fishing trip, with White Dove gathering her fishing net while Black Hawk retrieved his axe from the fur shed. Nicky would stay home and keep the woodstove company.

The couple left on the dogsled, Black Hawk mushing the dogs out onto the open lake. The huskies ran with gusto, an energy Black Hawk had not seen them exhibit before. The dogs were anxious to eat the protein their working bodies needed, knowing they were going fishing and looking forward to an all-you-can-eat buffet of fish.

Fifteen minutes later, the sled reached the holes in the ice used for fishing. Black Hawk reopened the holes with his axe, clearing the way for White Dove to place her net to catch fish. Two hours later, after feeding the dogs their fill of fish, the couple loaded a bumper catch of whitefish onto the sled and headed home. White Dove and Black Hawk were both happy after a successful afternoon of fishing.

CHAPTER THIRTY-FIVE

The month of January passed quickly, with the couple's days filled with trapping. Mornings were spent checking the trapline for fur caught the night before. Their catch was returned to the cabin and processed in the fur shed daily. A bounty of furs was harvested during the month, including beaver, bobcat, wolverine, and a lone, skinny wolf. That animal was the one who had escaped Black Hawk's bullet the last time he had visited their cabin. The starving animal had taken his chances, trying to steal the bait from the trap, which led to his death. Black Hawk thought that was a better way for the animal to die, rather than slowly dying of starvation.

The days during January were short and gray, with clouds dominating the winter sky. Black Hawk set snares to catch rabbits for food, as their supply of moose meat in the outdoor freezer was dwindling. Black Hawk thought about shooting a deer, knowing he could restock the outdoor freezer with enough meat to last the rest of the winter if he was successful. In the meantime, they both enjoyed rabbit and the snares proved to catch quite a few.

In late January, the couple were about to leave to check

the twenty traps on their trapline. The sled dogs were healthy, having been fed a diet of fish and the special blend of dry food Black Hawk had purchased while in Dawson. The dogs pulled hard on their harnesses, carrying the couple to the first stop on the trapline, which was empty. They continued checking their traps, harvesting a few common mammals, such as pine martens and weasels. Wanting to check their two beaver traps, Black Hawk steered the dog team toward the pond.

Beaver was not only valued for their fur, but the meat was a favorite of the trappers and functioned as a good substitute meal for the dogs, when the couple ran out of whitefish to feed the always hungry animals. Black Hawk mushed his dogs onto the frozen surface of the beaver pond. Arriving at the first trap, he could not believe what he was seeing. In the snow were footprints larger than any the couple had seen before. Black Hawk thought there was only one explanation for these oversized prints, they must belong to the legendary ape man who lives in the forests of Canada's north. Bigfoot was an elusive creature, rarely observed by humans in its forest habitat.

After finding both beaver traps empty, Black Hawk turned the sled dogs toward home, the thought of the giant footprints fresh in the couple's minds. Arriving back at their cabin without incident, Black Hawk and White Dove finished their never-ending work before retiring to their cabin for a quiet evening together. They enjoyed spending time with their dog, Nicky, a companion like no other in this frozen land located in Canada's north.

CHAPTER THIRTY-SIX

The month of February was like the month of January. Working the trapline, Black Hawk and White Dove harvested furs daily. The couple planned to work the trapline until the end of March. It was important to get the winter's harvest of furs to Dawson to be sold before the snow melted. If that were to happen, travel by dogsled would become obsolete, depriving Black Hawk of a reliable means of transportation until the following year.

If their trapping season continued to be a success, Black Hawk and White Dove would earn enough money to buy lumber from the sawmill. They wanted to use the lumber to build the addition onto the fur shed, which they hoped to build this summer. As the calendar changed to the month of March, the hours of daylight grew longer. The Yukon winter was slowly ending, giving way to the season of spring. Soon the forests would be full of birdsong and the lakes would be full of waterfowl, as life returned to this unforgiving land.

Black Hawk and White Dove cashed in their furs in late March, earning enough money to build the addition onto their shed and pay for their living expenses for the remainder of the year. The spring brought a sense of relief to the forest community living in the wilds of Canada's north. It was a season which brought hope to the trappers, who had just lived through another long winter. The barren land would soon be green again, with beautiful wildflowers covering the meadows in a sea of vibrant colours. It was a land which showed its true spirit, a land called the Yukon, Canada's treasure of the north.

ACKNOWLEDGEMENTS

Many thanks to Astrid, who managed to capture my picture of where the characters in my books lived with her map. She was a joy to work with and I believe she truly nailed my vision. And thanks to our son, Elijah, for his help in selecting the images depicting the true north.